AGELESS LOVE

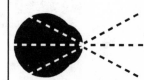

VIRGINIA WEDDINGS, BOOK 1

AGELESS LOVE

A ROMANCE PERSEVERES IN THE COMMONWEALTH

LAURALEE BLISS

THORNDIKE PRESS

An imprint of Thomson Gale, a part of The Thomson Corporation

Detroit • New York • San Francisco • New Haven, Conn. • Waterville, Maine • London

THOMSON

GALE

Thorndike Press® Large Print Christian Romance.

The text of this Large Print edition is unabridged.

Other aspects of the book may vary from the original edition.

Set in 16 pt. Plantin.

LIBRARY OF CONGRESS CATALOGING-IN-PUBLICATION DATA

Bliss, Lauralee.
    Ageless love : a romance perseveres in the commonwealth / by Lauralee Bliss.
        p. cm. — (Virginia weddings ; bk. #1) (Thorndike Press large print Christian romance)
    ISBN-13: 978-1-4104-0452-7 (alk. paper)
    ISBN-10: 1-4104-0452-8 (alk. paper)
    1. Man-woman relationships — Fiction. 2. Virginia — Fiction. 3. Large type books. I. Title.
PS3602.L575A35 2008
813'.6—dc22   2007042464

Published in 2008 by arrangement with Barbour Publishing, Inc.

Printed in the United States of America on permanent paper
10 9 8 7 6 5 4 3 2 1

DEAR READER,

What a beautiful area to kindle a romance — in sight of Virginia's mysterious yet awesome Blue Ridge Mountains. In *Virginia Weddings,* you are about to undertake a journey of the heart, soul, and spirit as couples, both young and old, solve mysteries while finding romance.

Just as I experienced love here on a mountain summit in Virginia some nineteen years ago, I welcome you to join these heroines and heroes who overcome their difficulties to discover enduring love within the realm of breathtaking and rejuvenating scenery. I hope their stories of faith will touch your life and fill you with the knowledge of God's unending love and concern for you.

I welcome you to visit my Web site at www .lauraleebliss.com to discover other books that will uplift your spirit while providing page-turning entertainment.

May God bless you.

Lauralee

Dedication

To my mom, Lucille Braun,
and her wonderful enthusiasm for
gardening
which I now enjoy so much.

CHAPTER 1

Daphne Elliot cringed at the melodious sound erupting from the storehouse. Rodney was at it again, serenading his work with song. He burst into a merry tune the moment he arrived for work in the morning. It unnerved her to see him floating on a cloud with a song of love on his lips — and from a young man to boot. "Tweet, tweet," she mumbled. "Love's sweet song, blah. A pain in the pinfeathers, I call it."

"I heard that, Miss Elliot," said Rodney James, who came in carrying several bags of lawn seed on his shoulder. He plopped the bags on the floor of the garden center with a grunt. "Sounds familiar."

"It's from the wise old owl in *Bambi*. I don't wear these glasses of mine just for seeing, you know. There's great wisdom in age."

Rodney leaned over the counter with a boyish grin plastered on his face. Shocks of wavy dark hair framed his thin face that

9

boasted luminous brown eyes. To Daphne, these young people seemed to be getting younger all the time.

"The problem with you, Miss Elliot, is that you aren't in love."

"You're quite mistaken, young man. I am very much in love." She picked up a feather duster and aimed it at the store shelves brimming with planting supplies, seed packets, fertilizers, insect control, and decorative planters. "With this, and this, and finally" — she pointed to a box of plant food — "this."

Rodney erupted into laughter, bringing a smile to Daphne's lips, which were colored a deep wine with swipes of her favorite lipstick. Despite the songs of love that permeated his work, Daphne enjoyed having the young man around. Rodney was prompt and helpful and did more around the nursery than anyone else she had ever hired. And he did it all without complaining.

She sighed, staring at the Garden Center Nursery that had been a part of her life since she was a young girl. It seemed unbelievable that she was still able to run this place. Her father opened the center back in the early 1950s. Normally a son would have inherited the family business, but her older brother, Charles, would have nothing to do with it. He lived out on the West Coast, far away from her home in Virginia. In fact, Daphne rarely heard from him other than the annual Christmas card that included a picture of him, surrounded by his children and grandchildren. When Daphne looked at the picture of Charles and his flock, she often wondered why life had passed her by. Then she would come back to the shop, work in the greenhouse, and find herself renewed. The feel of the cool dirt between her fingers and the flowers that bloomed from her efforts gave her a peace that this was where she was meant to be. Marriage and children were never a part of God's big plan for her life. This business was the plan, and the good Lord had prospered it far beyond her imagination.

Over the years, Daphne had many helpers come and go in the business. For a long time, she had a co-owner named Phyllis, an old friend from her high school days. She later became ill and had to leave. Daphne never once entertained the idea of a man becoming a co-owner. The men she preferred working at the shop had to be less than thirty years of age so they would do what she expected. They would be like sons receiving instructions from their matriarch, or so she liked to think.

By far Rodney had been the best of her previous employees. A lady at church recommended him. He had worked for Daphne in her garden shop just a short time before announcing his engagement to a young lady named Melanie. Six months later, they were married. A year had passed since then, and Rodney still carried a song of love on his lips. While Daphne disliked the connotation, she couldn't help but marvel at his beautiful singing voice. She informed him that he should try out for the summer theater program. Rodney only laughed and went off whistling another love song.

"There must be somebody I can fix you up with," Rodney said now, adjusting the sign advertising the lawn seed for sale.

With the spring planting season underway, Daphne made certain the store had a good supply of lawn seed. Many customers came in, complaining that the winter weather had killed their grass, the dreaded crabgrass had taken over like an invading army, or the heat of the past summer had steamed their lawns to a drab brown.

"How about in your church?" Rodney continued.

"Really, the only thing that needs fixing up around here is the sign for my store, which you promised to do yesterday."

"I'll go get the ladder. The hammer and nails are —"

"In the back on the workbench." Daphne returned to tidying up the counter after a long day of sales. Spring was the busiest time of the year, with everyone seeking to turn their property into bountiful gardens of flowers or fresh produce. Daphne had to bite her tongue when one customer came in asking for tomato plants. She patiently explained that it was too early to plant them now and she must wait for the last frost to be over. The bewildered customer chose packets of tomato seeds then and said she would grow her own. Daphne kept any further comments to herself. She was far too outspoken anyway.

At home she had no one to debate her daily struggles in life with but her dog, Chubs. Most evenings, the dog lay at her feet with his mouth hanging open, waiting for her to scratch his belly or throw him dog biscuits. Daphne never thought she would live her life as a spinster, but that must be the way God wanted it. Perhaps He knew no one could live with her tongue. Yet she refused to believe the good things in life had passed her by, even when gazing at her brother's many children and grandchildren. *There's more to life than marriage and children,* she told herself. *It all depends on how you look at it. And I'm going to be content right where I am.*

The bell to the door tinkled at that moment. Daphne looked at the clock and frowned. She had forgotten to turn the sign on the door, signaling that the shop was closed for the day. In the door walked a typical farmer of the region, dressed in dirty overalls with grass sticking to his knees, wearing a straw hat. A strange scar lay near the corner of his right eye, encompassing the right side of his cheek and extending to his neck. She wondered what could have caused such a scar. He did not look her way but scanned the aisles as if trying to decide what he wanted. Daphne stood watching his uncertainty for a moment before asking if she could help.

"I want to plant a flower garden," he said, "but I don't know how."

Oh dear. This is going to make me close up late. What will I do about Chubs who must be let out on time or he'll have an accident?

At that moment Rodney came in, lugging a small stepladder. He struggled with it, nearly losing his grip and bumping the ladder into the farmer's legs. He managed a smile and headed out the door. Daphne wanted to inform the man that she was about to close up shop and ask if he'd come back tomorrow. Instead, she came out from behind the counter. "Follow me." She proceeded to point out the various materials he would need to prepare a flower bed — humus, peat moss, fertilizer.

"I need all that just for flowers?" he asked, scratching a mound of gray hair beneath the straw hat he wore.

"It's important if you want your investment to survive. If you want to dig a few holes in this awful soil we have and throw in a few plants, you'll have a garden for about a week."

He raised an eyebrow. "You've got a lot of spunk there."

Daphne felt the heat rise in her cheeks. *And you have a lot of nerve coming in here when I'm about to close.* She clamped her mouth shut to keep the words from escaping. "It's been a long day, and I'm closing."

"I'm sorry. You looked as if you were open, and the sign there says —"

"Yes, I know. I forgot to turn it." Daphne pushed back a wisp of gray hair. "If you would like any of the materials I was telling you about, Rodney here will gladly help load them into your car." She glanced over to see a rustic truck parked in the lot, with mud up to the middle of the wheels. Wherever he lived, the place was hip-deep in mud, not uncommon with the spring rains. "Spring is actually an excellent time to put in a garden, with the soil nice and moist. I usually begin my flower seeds in February, replant them in small pots, then put them out in the greenhouse to harden them off. I have some excellent varieties here at the nursery that should do well, depending on where you wish to plant them."

The farmer crossed his arms and leaned against the side of the shop. "Well, I want to plant flowers in my front yard, you see."

"I'm certain your wife will enjoy looking at them out the window."

"I'm sure she would if she were alive. She died five years ago."

Daphne looked away. Rodney again peered at her, this time wearing a slight smile on his face. She could almost hear his thoughts. *Aha! An eligible widower and in your age range.* How she would love to shake that young man for grinning like a cat who nipped the canary, or more like Cupid ready to shoot the arrow. "I'm sorry to hear that."

"Thank you. I miss her, but I'm finding out the hard way that I can get along in life on my own."

She felt an internal sigh of relief creep up within her. At least he had not come here with some ulterior motive. She'd had a few customers in her day who sought more than just planting material or a healthy evergreen tree. They were also on the prowl. She would not soon forget Larson McCall a year ago. He had been congenial, offering her advice about her nursery, even taking her to the Hardware Store Restaurant for dinner. Only when Rodney found out the man intended to steal her business did she realize how close she had come to disaster, and all because of a yearning within her to enjoy the company of a man. Between the loss she'd suffered when she was young and the duping by Larson when she was older, she wanted to stay far away from any hint of a relationship. "Well, we have many varieties that will look wonderful in a garden spot. Of course, you also need to decide if you want annuals that only live a season or perennials that will bloom year after year."

"What would you say?"

"I like both. I plant different annuals each year. Perennials will come up in the same place I plant them. Since annuals live only a season, you can change the varieties." Daphne began showing him the different plants for sale. When she glanced up, she found his gaze centered not on plants but on her. Daphne felt her face grow warm and a strange flutter begin in her chest. Her heart was acting up again. Soon she would have to sit down and put her feet up, as the doctor had ordered on her last exam. "Excuse me, Mr. —"

"Jack McNary."

"Mr. McNary, I'm afraid I'll have to stop now. I'm getting a little tired. If you want anything, Rodney will be glad to help you."

A look of concern flashed across his rugged face, decorated with sparse wrinkles. His bushy gray eyebrows lowered over a set of ice blue eyes. "Are you all right?"

"It's been a long day."

"I'm mighty sorry. I'll come back tomorrow. When do you open?"

"Nine a.m."

He tipped his large straw hat at her. "Nine a.m.," he said, as if setting up some kind of date, then strode off toward the truck.

Rodney came down from the ladder and whistled while twirling the hammer. "Miss Elliot, now that was a D.E. if ever I saw one."

Daphne knew what he meant. *Divine Encounter.* In her eyes, she saw nothing divine about it — just a customer wanting a few posies to spruce up an otherwise dreary life.

In fact, he was no different from her, though she hated to admit it. "Help me close up, Rodney. I'm feeling those chest pains again."

"I'll close up. You go on home and rest."

She smiled her thanks. That was another good quality of Rodney. She could trust him with closing the store tighter than a drum and making sure the money was locked in the safe. She was thankful she had already finished the books for the day. Rodney offered to do the bookkeeping on his computer at home, but Daphne preferred the old-fashioned way, in a long memo book. In the back of the store, she kept her father's books, etched in his stately handwriting. Occasionally he had allowed her to do the books as a young woman. Daphne marveled at how her writing had changed little with the passage of time, even if her heart acted up on her. At times she astonished young Rodney with her sharp memory when it came to ordering supplies for the store. Rodney told her she was a walking computer and could probably give the customers their change without using a cash register.

Daphne inserted the key into the door of her home, situated a mile from the nursery. Inside she heard Chubs barking his customary greeting, which also indicated his eagerness to go out. "Yes, I hear you," she told him, taking the red leash off a hook near the door. The dog, a medium-sized mutt of mixed breeds with a stomach that sagged near the ground, wagged his tail furiously as she hooked the leash to his collar.

Outside, a cool spring breeze blew. From her porch Daphne could look out across the busy street to the wide expanse of the Blue Ridge Mountains stretched out lazily before her. She enjoyed these spring evenings when the mountains shone crystal clear, displaying all their glory. When summer came, the haze would often mar the view she had come to love since she was a child.

The property Daphne owned once belonged to the Elliot family, but now she was the sole proprietor with brother Charles off in another state raising his family. Both her parents were long gone, as were numerous aunts and uncles. Daphne realized that with the passage of time came the pain of losing friends and family members once close to her. It gave her a deeper understanding of how fragile life could be and left her considering her own time remaining on earth. What would she do about the house and the business if she were to pass on suddenly? If she left it to Charles, he would sell it all in a heartbeat.

She then thought of ambitious, love-struck Rodney. He would make a fine business-man, if he could keep his head on earth and out of the clouds. If he took over the busi-ness, then he and his wife, Melanie, could live here instead of that crowded apartment. Daphne coaxed Chubs back into the small home. She would ask the young man about it. If he agreed, she would call her lawyer and make the arrangements.

Daphne went into the kitchen and looked in the cupboards, ready for her old standby — a can of soup — for dinner. It made no sense for her to cook elaborate meals when she was the only one to eat it. Sometimes she invited the ladies from church over for a meal and even once had Rodney and Mela-nie to dinner, but she found little interest in cooking for one person. *It's too much of a bother,* she would argue, and usually the argumentative side won out. Daphne reached for her favorite flavor, chicken and rice, and began heating it over the circle of blue flame on the gas stove.

The ruffle of fur at her legs sent her glanc-ing downward at Chubs. He was wagging his tail politely. "No soup for you," Daphne told him. She opened a can of dog food and spooned it into a plastic bowl, which Chubs downed in several healthy bites.

When the soup was warm, she carried it over to the table, pulled out the evening paper, and began reading. This was the typical nightly fare — a dinner of soup or some other quick dish, and the evening paper to go along with it. Then she would sit in the family room to work on a bit of embroidery while watching a game show, or she would catch up on a favorite mystery novel. Afterward she would read her Bible, then climb into bed promptly at nine. Nothing swayed her schedule unless it was a matter of life and death. Daphne had to be on a schedule, or those pains in her chest would rise up to remind her.

After glancing through the newspaper, Daphne washed out her bowl, then moseyed over to the sitting room and turned on a lamp. She looked at her embroidery and her mystery novel, but neither of them interested her. Instead, her gaze fell on several old photo albums collecting dust on the bookshelf. Her hand shook slightly as she reached out and withdrew one. Dust bunnies flew. Daphne settled herself in a worn chair and opened the pages with a slight creaking sound. The white background where the photos rested was now yellowed with age. She had put these pictures in the albums close to fifteen years ago. They had been a jumbled mess in her bedroom drawer until she'd finally decided one day to take them out and arrange them in the albums.

Now she began opening each page, tracing the people in the pictures with her finger. The Great Smoky Mountains of Tennessee. A yellow framed house. A harvest festival. She paused at a page and stared. Piles of lumber occupied the background. And there he was — young, handsome Henry Morgan, similar to Rodney with his enthusiasm for life and for love. He had bushy black hair, a trimmed beard, and blue eyes. And he loved working with the trees. Working as a lumberjack was his trade. He and the trees were similar — strong, able to withstand harsh storms, giving shade and protection when the fierce summer sun came forth. He was her shelter and her love until he was cruelly taken away one dreadful day.

Even after all these years, the tears still gathered in her eyes. How could he have died, leaving her alone to face life? She shut the book when a wave of pain filtered through her chest. Her hand fumbled on the stand for the bottle of medicine that the doctor had prescribed for these symptoms. She placed one under her tongue. *I can't keep doing this. It's been forty years, and nothing has changed. Henry is dead . . . even though I was never able to wear my wedding dress or hold his arm while walking up the aisle of the church. Our children died with him. I can't do anything but forget.* If only she could.

CHAPTER 2

Daphne drove up to the nursery the next morning only to find the mud-drenched truck parked in the lot. Jack McNary sat behind the wheel, reading the morning newspaper. She glanced at her watch. There he was, right on time. She was a little late this morning, having slept in after suffering a restless night's sleep. She knew better than to stare at old photographs before going to bed. The memories were carried into her dreams, even though they should be locked in a closet and the key thrown away.

Daphne walked into the shop and found Rodney inside counting out the cash to place in the register. "Miss Elliot, he refused to come in."

"What?" she asked, a bit flustered.

"Your buddy out there. He was here when I came, but he wouldn't enter the store until —" Rodney didn't finish his sentence but instead waved his hand. "Good morning."

"Morning," said Jack McNary. He stepped inside holding a brown paper bag.

"I need to go check on some products in the storehouse," Rodney said, sidestepping away, but not before giving Daphne that grin she always detested.

She went behind the counter, trying hard not to look at the farmer's face.

"I brought you breakfast," he announced, holding up the bag.

Daphne jerked her head up, and at once her glasses slipped down her nose. She pushed them up with her finger. He wore a grin that sent wrinkles running through the huge blanket of scar tissue across his right cheek. "You what?"

"I brought breakfast. An egg biscuit from the convenience store down the road. And coffee. I don't know if you like any of those fancy coffees. Me, well, I like it strong and black, with none of those fancy flavors like hazelnut."

"Thank you, but I don't drink coffee. It gives me heartburn. And I don't eat eggs either. Too much cholesterol. Besides, I had my oatmeal." She turned and reached for the apron she liked to wear over her clothing.

"Sorry about that. I should have known."

"You had no way of knowing. There's no

sense in apologizing for it."

"After I heard you complaining yesterday about feeling worn-out and all, I thought maybe you might have some kind of heart condition. We aren't spring chickens anymore. The old ticker can sometimes wreak havoc when you least expect it."

Daphne tried to conceal her flushed face. She couldn't believe how close the man had come to discovering her ailment, as if he could look right through her. Heart conditions ran in Daphne's family. Her father died young from a heart ailment. And Daphne had recently been diagnosed with high blood pressure — not that any of these situations cropping up in her life were helping in that area. "Mr. McNary, can we help you get your items for the garden? I would love to chat, but I have a lot of work to do."

Jack folded the top of the bag. "Good. Glad to hear you want to chat. Maybe I can come back after you close up shop, and we can sit a spell."

Again she felt a pain rippling in her chest. It was too much to bear. Surely the man had devious intentions, like that Larson character. "Pardon me." She went outside to the storage shed where Rodney's singing filtered out the door. "Rodney, please take care of Mr. McNary."

"Miss Elliot!"

"I mean it. Tell him I had to do something. My heart can't take it."

"What did he do?"

"I — well, I don't know. Just take care of his needs. I'm having chest pains again."

Rodney nodded and took her hand in his, giving a gentle squeeze. "Miss Elliot, you just need to open up that heart of yours a little. Maybe if you did, it wouldn't hurt so much." He winked and strode back to the store, whistling another love song.

Daphne trembled at the truth of his words. She peeked out the window of the storehouse to see Rodney and the farmer going through the stacks of planting material. She then saw him give Rodney the paper bag containing the egg biscuit. If only she hadn't been so curt. He was just being polite, but right now the thought of another man wishing to spend time with her was enough to send her to bed for a week. She had the stress of the business, after all. She couldn't take the stress of a relationship on top of it, especially when she barely knew him.

Before he left the store, Jack came lumbering over to her, his hands planted inside his dirty overalls — the same pair he wore yesterday, no doubt. "I just wanted to apologize for making you so uncomfortable. Really, all I wanted to do was chat about plants. The biscuit I brought was only a peace offering after making you stay open late on account of me. Nothing more."

Daphne blinked. Perhaps she had been hasty in her judgment and the man wanted only to learn from a plant specialist. Maybe it was Rodney who had inflated the whole encounter, enough to where she nearly had to take more of her medicine. "I appreciate your saying that. If you would like to come back and discuss gardening, I'd gladly arrange it."

With the smile that erupted on his face, Daphne thought she had invited him to a fried-chicken dinner complete with apple pie.

"I'd like that, thank you. I haven't yet bought the plants, so I would like your opinion on them. When would be a good time?"

"Come by around five o'clock."

Jack lifted his straw hat, said a pleasant thank-you, and strode out to his muddy truck. Daphne looked out the window as the truck pulled away.

"There — you see?" Rodney said with a saucy grin on his face. "That wasn't so hard."

"You read too much into things, young man," she said, returning to the counter. "We are only going to discuss gardening. Nothing more."

Rodney leaned over the counter. "And I know that the best way for a man to meet a woman is to share some common interest. That's how I met Melanie. She liked to hang out in craft stores, looking for posies to make those silk flower arrangements."

"She does a wonderful job. You're blessed to have her." While Daphne enjoyed live flowers more, the pretty silk flower arrangement Melanie had made for her last Christmas brightened up her home during the dreary winter months. Other times of the year, Daphne cut real flowers from her own garden to add color to the house.

"So I pretended I was interested in painting," he continued. "The art supplies were in the next aisle over from the fake flowers. She was standing there one day, trying to decide what flowers she wanted, and we happened to bump into each other. It was love at first sight. It can happen to anyone, at any time, and at any age."

"I don't know about you. It seems to me you always have something up your sleeve. You're definitely one who likes to plan mysteries."

"I only like to solve mysteries in people's lives, Miss Elliot."

She chuckled. "You'll never solve mine, young man."

The look in his eye made her nervous. "Is that a challenge?"

"Yes. I'm challenging you to do your work. We have a business to run."

He gave a wink before striding off to the back room to finish unpacking the goods that had arrived by truck. The words were disconcerting to Daphne. *As if I don't have enough to think about in life without wondering what that young man is up to.* Somehow she had to convince Rodney she didn't need or want a man, nor did she want to be involved in some mysterious plot he contrived. She wanted to be left alone with her shop, her flowers, and her memories.

Despite the rocky start, the day had turned out pleasant but busy, with many customers coming by for their spring planting necessities. With the way she and Rodney scurried around the place, trying to fill customers' needs, Daphne wondered if she might need to hire extra help to ease the burden. She was thankful most of the customers knew what they wanted, which made life easier. A few had questions about specific gardening material or plants suitable for certain locations. The cash register rang endlessly. Now Daphne sat at the counter, hunched over the long memo book, adding up the day's totals. Rodney had already said good-bye, announcing he was taking Melanie out to her favorite Chinese restaurant. Daphne waved him off, but not before thanking him for his help.

She had just put down a long series of numbers, ready to tally them up, when a knock came on the door. After Rodney left for the day, Daphne always closed the shop up tight, along with turning the sign and locking the dead bolt. She peered between some shelving to see Jack McNary standing there, waiting expectantly. Daphne sighed. She'd forgotten she had told him to return at five o'clock after the shop had closed. She wondered if she should let him in without Rodney there. Daphne decided to ignore him and went back to doing the figures. The knocking persisted until suddenly she saw his face peer into a window near the counter. The image nearly made her faint.

She leaped to her feet and came to the door. "You scared me half to death!"

"I thought maybe you'd forgotten about our chat."

"I'm right in the middle of doing my books."

"I'm good at math," he said.

"So am I." She watched the look on his face change from one of expectation to obvious disappointment. Immediately her cold nature began to melt. If there was one thing she couldn't stand, it was seeing a sad face, especially one generated by some foolish statement that had escaped out of her mouth. "You can stay for a few minutes." She opened the door.

Jack took off his straw hat and stepped inside. Shiny gray hair stood up wildly on end. He smelled like the fields. He followed Daphne over to the counter where she had begun adding up the figures on paper. "Don't you have a calculator?"

"No, I don't."

"Be right back." Jack placed the hat on his head and headed out to his truck, returning with a calculator. "Okay, you read the numbers off, and I'll punch them in. We'll get this done in no time."

"Actually I prefer doing it myself." If the truth were known, she didn't want him discovering the amount of money they had made that day. He might be here to rob her blind, just like Larson McCall. He had been a sweet talker, too, but under it all lay a cold, crooked heart. For all she knew, Jack's offer of the calculator was only a guise for something evil lurking within, only to leap out when she least expected it.

A shiver raced through her. She looked around for the telephone in case she needed to dial 911. Rodney had told her many times she should get a cell phone, especially if she was here working late or at least while driving around in the car. Daphne turned up her nose at the suggestion. Young people were forever throwing electronic gadgets in her face. Computers, cell phones, everything.

"Sorry. I was only trying to help." He pocketed the calculator and looked around. "I hope you still have time to tell me more about gardening. I'm sure you know everything."

"I do know quite a bit, and it would take much longer than the time I have to explain it. I think I told you yesterday what you would need for your garden. There isn't much else to discuss."

"If you could point out the plants that would be good, I'll pick them up. That is, unless your assistant is around to help me."

Daphne opened her mouth, ready to tell him he was long gone, then thought better of it. Instead, she led Jack around the nursery. When they came to the plants, Daphne began to relax. These living things were like her children, and who wouldn't want to boast about one's children? She picked up a pack of petunias, gently stroking the velvety petals. "Petunias are one of my favorites. They come in such wonderful colors and never fail to brighten my day. I also like rosebushes, but they're bug babies."

"Why is that?"

"Every bug and disease seem to love them. They must be treated right. They require proper fertilizing and pruning, and then they require different chemicals to treat them." She showed him the chemicals to manage the diseases of black spot and powdery mildew. "And then in June, we get those dreadful Japanese beetles. They chew everything."

"I heard about them. Chewed a good many of my apple trees one year and also my climbing rose. I hung those beetle traps, but it didn't work."

"The traps only make more come, usually from your neighbor's yard."

Jack crossed his arms before him. "Is that a fact?"

"They are actually quite easy to pick off, if you don't mind the feel of them, that is."

"I can't imagine a lady like you handling bugs."

Daphne gritted her teeth at the insinuation that she couldn't handle things. "I take care of all kinds of bugs, large and small."

Jack only smiled.

"I even killed a black widow spider on my property," she added, lifting her head higher. She would show him he was not talking to a limp weed, even if her heart did act up on occasion. She was as tough as an oak tree, all things considered.

"Is that a fact? You shouldn't fool around with those. They're highly poisonous, you know."

"Everything can kill nowadays. You could step into that truck and meet your end right there on Highway 29."

"I can't argue with that. I'm sure glad I know where I'm going. I'd hate to be someone who didn't know where he was going if I were to up and die like that. You think of people who die in accidents and such, and who knows if they've gotten right with the Lord. Makes my hair stand up just thinking about it. Like when that crazy lunatic was shooting up all those folks awhile back. They were shopping and pumping gas and all; then a bullet cuts them down. You never know when it's going to be your time." He relaxed his arms. "But I'm sure you know where you're going, right, Miss Elliot?"

"If you don't mind, right now I really need to go home. I have a dog to let out. He has accidents if I'm not there."

"I won't take up any more of your time. You just tell me how much this is going to cost." Along with several boxes of petunias, he added some decorative pots, rose chemicals, and several bags of fertilizer.

Daphne walked into the store and to the cash register. When the final total rang up to $40.14, she decided the extra effort was worth it. "I'll carry out a box of plants," she offered, observing Jack lift up the rest of the material he had bought. She marveled at his strength. No doubt hard work had put muscle on the man's body. Henry had the best muscles around from his work as a lumberjack. She used to love running her fingers over his hefty biceps, and he loved displaying them, too.

The thought made her flush. How could she think of such things, and especially with Jack McNary standing there? The box of plants began to tremble in her hands.

He opened the hatch to the bed of the truck, and she carefully placed the plants inside. "I sure would love to have you show me where to plant the flowers," he said, more to himself than to her.

Daphne's mouth fell open. "I hope you're not suggesting I go to your home and plant these? I'm not a landscaper, you know, though I can give you the name of a good one in town. I have enough to do trying to manage this business."

"I was only making a suggestion. I thought you would take it as a compliment." He loaded in the last of the bags beside the plants. Without another word, he entered the driver's seat.

Daphne walked back to the store, but not before casting a glance over her shoulder. She could plainly see his irritation. Again her mouth had taken over the situation as it always did. She doubted she would ever see him again. Did it really matter? Inwardly she should be thankful. God might have spared her further calamity in her life. Yet some interesting characteristics about Jack McNary drew her. He was polite and caring, for one thing. How many men did she know who would come bearing a breakfast sandwich as a peace offering? He had nice manners. Daphne always judged people on their manners. He had apologized more to her in the past two days than she had in her lifetime.

Daphne shook her head. She couldn't possibly find herself wrapped up with another man. She would not be left on a stoop wearing her bridal gown smudged with dirt, the tears causing wrinkles on the bodice of the gown, while men died or left town with all her money. She had been down that road. Time did not heal the wounds. Neither did her work in the nursery with the plants she lovingly tended. What then could heal them?

CHAPTER 3

"I think it would do you good to go. Miss Elliot, are you listening to me?"

Daphne wished she had a set of earplugs to tune out that young man while she tried to keep occupied in the greenhouse, repotting the summer vegetables. She had ordered Rodney to work at the counter in the hope of keeping his convicting words out of earshot. He continued to insist that she come Sunday afternoon for a picnic at his church. Daphne disliked eating lunch with perfect strangers, even if they were good Christians. She sat with a few ladies she knew at her church on Sunday but rarely did much socializing.

Rodney often talked about his church, the same place where she had witnessed him and Melanie exchange their marital vows. The pastor had been amiable enough. The church was clean and neat, and the people friendly. But visiting foreign churches made her nervous. She only went to the wedding out of respect for Rodney. In fact, to Daphne's embarrassment, Melanie had a picture of Daphne, Rodney, and her blown up and framed. It now sat in a prominent position in the young couple's living room.

"You're like a mother to Rodney," Melanie said with a smile. "It means a lot to both of us."

Daphne wasn't certain whether to take this as a compliment or not. Now it appeared she was expected to attend other events at Rodney's church, including this Spring Fling — or whatever he called it.

"You'll get some nice fresh air," Rodney continued, "and eat a wonderful lunch in the great outdoors."

"With the ants and flies," she added curtly.

None of her arguments dissuaded the young man. When Daphne returned to the greenhouse, Rodney followed, helping her open a large bag of premium potting soil. Daphne's fingers were already at work in the soft soil, ready to place the delicate plants inside their new potted homes. "I'll have Melanie make a great dessert if you come," he said. "Maybe some fruited gelatin."

"I'm the one who makes a good fruited

salad, if you remember," Daphne reminded him.

"Great! I'll tell everyone you'll be bringing a fruited salad to the picnic. The kids will love you."

Daphne spun around, her fingers caked with soil. "Young man —," she began, only to see him disappear into the store with the echo of a song trailing him. *Oh, he irritates me to no end. If he weren't such a good helper, I would get someone else. But that would be foolish. There's no one else like him. Without him, this place would wither away and me along with it.* Daphne inhaled a few breaths to calm herself, knowing that if she didn't, the heart pains would greet her once again.

The tinkle of the store bell alerted her to a customer. Daphne continued repotting tiny squash plants, barely able to make out the conversation in the shop. This was what she enjoyed doing the most, immersing herself in the work of repotting plants. She scooped out more soil onto the worktable; then out of the corner of her eye, she saw a dark figure hover over her. Her trowel went airborne. The dirt landed squarely in Jack McNary's face and straw hat. He stared, bewildered, like a child with chocolate on his face. Particles of dirt rolled off the brim of his hat.

"Oh no," Daphne moaned and gave him some paper towels. "You shouldn't sneak up on me like that."

"I didn't mean to startle you. I was here to get more dirt, and I guess I did." He cracked a grin. "What are you doing?" He pointed at the array of plants and their bare roots, laid out on newspaper. "Won't they die like that?"

"They would if they stay in the same pots where I planted them as seeds. The seedlings are now becoming root-bound. I'm repotting them into bigger containers."

"I've never seen plants like that, all naked and everything." He turned red. "What I mean is, you know, out of the ground like that, just lying there. I thought they couldn't survive."

"You must work quickly and give them plenty of water after they are repotted." Daphne picked up a small plant to show him the new roots. "See what pure white roots they have? Baby roots, just like a newborn. Fragile and in need of care. I just put my thumb into the soil like this and then slip the plant inside."

Jack stared, watching her every move. "You have a way with plants, Miss Elliot. I told you that you should have planted mine.

I killed pretty near all of them. That's another reason I'm here — to buy more plants."

Daphne whirled to face him. The news stunned her. How could he have killed the plants — and so soon? "Oh no. What did you do?"

"I thought I had some time before they went into the ground, you see. It takes time to get the soil ready, as you told me. I had to dig it all up. Then I had to wait to rent a rototiller. I don't have one of my own. The fellow at the store said there would be one, but it didn't show up for three days. By the time I got the ground ready, pretty near all the plants were dead."

Daphne shook her head. She placed her hands on her hips, unaware of the dirty markings she was making on her apron. "Mr. McNary, did you by chance water them?"

"Huh? You mean water them in their little pots?"

"Of course! In the small pots we use, the plants easily dry out in this spring sun. You have to water them every other day. More if it gets warm out."

"You didn't tell me that," he began, then quickly added, "but I should've figured it out."

Daphne lowered her arms, only to find her hips now blackened with the dirt. She felt a familiar heat rise in her face. They looked like a pair from a comedy routine — Jack with his dirty face and her with dirty hips. "I can't believe you would let the poor things dry out like that."

"I can tell you I take better care of people than plants," he said swiftly. "In fact, I make an awfully good barbecue. People from all around have commented on it. Stick-to-the-ribs kind, too."

"I suppose that's nice if you have a good heart and low blood pressure, which I don't have." Daphne returned to her duty. "I'm sorry, but I must get back to this before the plants dry out."

He stood there for several moments, watching her work. His observing gaze made her nervous. She wasn't used to being on display like this, especially in front of a man who didn't know enough to water plants. How could he have done that? If only she had accepted his offer to go to his home and take care of the gardening. The sweet plants would be alive and well, ready to face the morning sunshine and even a terrific summer storm. He would've had a garden people could be proud of.

Jack made a few more comments about

his barbecue that had won a prize at a cook-off. When she didn't respond, he planted his hands inside the pockets of his overalls and meandered back into the store. Rodney and he conversed for awhile longer. Daphne cast a glance inside the store, and Rodney looked at her and smiled. She quickly turned away. *I can't stand this. He truly thinks that Jack might be someone I should get to know. Dear Lord, please help me.*

At last Daphne heard the bells tinkle and the door close. On the worktable lay the paper towels he'd used to wipe the grime off his face. Daphne gathered them up, ready to toss them away. She stared at the paper towels and for some reason thought of Henry. Dear Henry, who accidentally upset her mother's dish of fine blackberry jam all over his lap. Daphne had rushed to find him some cloths to clean up the spill. Dark jam was everywhere.

"Now you have to kiss me," he told her. "You'll never find anyone sweeter than at this moment." And his kisses were sweet, better than clover honey, better than any dessert she could have tasted. She didn't care that he had spilt the jam. She only wanted him forever.

Daphne shook her head at the thought before discarding the paper towels in the wastebasket. She would do better to toss the memories away, too, rather than clinging to them. She should bury them deep, even burn them, anything to free her mind and her heart.

Daphne didn't know why she scooped up packages of gelatin from the shelf inside her favorite grocery store. Nor did she understand why she reached for several large cans of fruit cocktail and placed them in her cart. She had told Rodney a firm "no" to this Spring Fling at his church and even reiterated the point that very afternoon while closing up shop. Yet somehow, she felt moved to go to the store and buy the fixings for her famous recipe, just in case. After selecting a few more items, including dog food for Chubs, she rolled the cart to the checkout counter.

"Glad to see you again, Miss Elliot," said a young girl with black hair. Daphne couldn't remember her name, but she did recall that the girl had commented on a pair of old earrings she'd worn one day to the store. Daphne thought she needed glasses. The gold plating had long since chipped away, revealing the metal beneath. But they were earrings Henry had given her, and she'd worn them faithfully every Tuesday for the last forty years.

"Looks like you're going to make a fruited gelatin. My grandma used to make the best. She would put it out with the main meal, and we would always go for it rather than the rest of the dinner. There's nothing better."

Daphne fumbled for her wallet inside her purse. "Well, I've been invited to a Spring Fling, whatever, at my employee's church. I don't know if I'm going or not, but I thought I would get the ingredients together for it in case I changed my mind."

"It's supposed to be beautiful weather for a picnic," the girl said with a wink.

Daphne nearly believed Rodney had told this girl what to say in an effort to convince her to come. Or maybe it was God with another D.E. in her life. When she left the store, following the clerk who placed the bag in the trunk of her car, she considered the idea of a picnic in the great outdoors. While she loved plants, she was not much of an outdoor, picnic-type person. Still, Rodney might be right. Maybe she did need to get out of the stuffy places she had neatly constructed for herself and experience life anew. After all, the years were slipping away. With the way her health was these days, she might not even be able to enjoy the outdoors much longer. She would likely regret it if she didn't go, like other things she regretted in life.

Daphne arrived home and began at once to boil water for the gelatin. She retrieved from the cupboard her biggest mold with leaves carved into it. She had put on many a dinner party in her younger days, serving a fruited salad on a bed of crisp lettuce to the delight of visitors and family. Now she couldn't recall the last time she'd used the mold. Like most of the objects in her house, it had not been used in years. Daphne stirred up the gelatin and, when it began to thicken, added the drained fruit cocktail and chopped walnuts. For the last ingredient, she folded in a container of whipped cream and scooped it all into the mold to chill overnight.

Daphne wandered back to her closet to look for an appropriate picnic outfit. The closet was jammed with clothes from every year since she was a teenager. She hadn't thrown anything out, though she had been tempted several times to give garments away to the Salvation Army. She had clothing from every style of the twentieth century and even found clothes that had come back in fashion, like bell-bottoms and miniskirts. *It just shows how long I've been alive on this earth, when styles are already being recirculated in the twenty-first century.* She sorted through the clothes until she came to an evening dress, hidden away in a dark recess of the closet. Her hands began to tremble. Ever so slowly, she drew out the midnight blue, floor-length dress. She had worn this dress to a very special party, along with the pearl necklace and earrings Henry had given her at a Christmas party. That night she and Henry danced under the stars. It was a perfect evening, one for the storybooks.

Daphne stepped over to the mirror and held the dress up in front of her. In her reflection, she saw her face hovering above the elegant dress. Tiny wrinkles had begun to appear where she'd once had velvety-smooth skin. Henry loved to caress her cheek with his hand. Tears welled up in her eyes and dripped down her cheeks.

"I love the pearls you gave me," Daphne had told Henry that night. Her fingers touched each one, feeling their soft roundness. To her they were pearls of great price, though certainly not the greatest price.

"They are beautiful around your neck," he'd said, fingering the necklace before tracing a line across her cheek. The sensation sent chills running down her spine. He picked up her hand, and they waltzed to the music. Most young people then were embracing rock-and-roll tunes. Not Henry. He was like Daphne, preferring the waltz with an orchestra supplying the music. A walk in the moonlight topped off the evening. They stopped on a wooden bridge over a glistening river, with the shadowy line of Tennessee mountains framing the gray horizon. She'd told him that tomorrow she would have to return to Virginia. The nursery and the plants were calling her. He pulled her close and told her that one day he would return to Virginia and marry her.

That time never came. It died as he did — burned to ashes in the flames of a terrible fire that stole away his life and her happiness.

Daphne returned the gown to its rightful place in the back of her closet, among the other possessions she had gathered over the years. Now she concentrated on her newer fashions and pulled out a lavender pantsuit. The sleeves would need fixing, which she planned to do right now while she thought of it. Trotting over to the chair, she sat down and took out the sewing kit she kept inside an old cookie tin. It was so like her to take clothes out of the closet, even ones she had worn in the past, and alter them somehow.

Move a button there; change the length of a hem here. She didn't like the sleeves hanging over her wrists so she couldn't see the face on her watch. She first tried on the garment and measured the length, then set to work hemming up the sleeves.

The clock struck nine. Though she was tired, for some reason, she didn't want to go to bed. There were nights when Daphne feared crawling into bed and drifting off to sleep, wondering if she would wake up. With her heart acting up the way it did, she had no idea whether the Lord would keep her going to see another sunrise. Not that she had much to look forward to. Tomorrow was another day, but one in which she would meet strange people at a church picnic and eat her lunch with ants crawling along the tablecloth.

Daphne crossed the room and hung up the pantsuit. Chubs followed at her heels to his place in the corner of her bedroom and a large pillow Daphne had bought him for Christmas. The dog performed his usual routine — turning himself around three times before settling on the pillow for the night. And Daphne did her usual routine, as well — washing her face, brushing her teeth, and slipping on a nightgown before heading to bed. Tonight her mind was consumed with worry over the picnic tomor-row. Why did she ever listen to that foolish young man? Perhaps she could still get out of going. After all, she had not promised Rodney she would be there. But what would she do with that huge fruit salad she had made? Daphne shook her head and turned out the light. No doubt God must be chuck-ling at the myriad of questions that brought about more needless anxiety. She needed to trust Him with the small things as well as the big.

Daphne grimaced at the bright sunshine peeking through her window early the next morning. She had hoped it might rain and thus give her an excuse to stay home from the picnic. Instead she dressed, walked Chubs, and made a bowl of hot oatmeal for breakfast. She decided to forgo her own church service that morning, thinking it would be too difficult to go to her church first and then some strange church for lunch. Rather, she would watch a church program on television and attend the picnic at noon.

When the clock struck eleven, Daphne changed into the lavender pantsuit. In an afterthought, she put on the pearl necklace and earrings. She hadn't worn the necklace in years but felt sentimental today. After saying good-bye to Chubs, she took up the plate of fruited salad resting on a bed of lettuce leaves and gingerly went to her car.

The day was spectacular, with the Blue Ridge Mountains of Virginia clearly visible in the distance. It was days like this that Daphne wanted to be in the garden, feeling the cool soil between her fingers while planting rows of vegetable seeds. God's green earth beckoned to her with a persistence she usually could not ignore. But for now, only the picnic occupied her mind. She was determined to make it through these few hours, come what may.

Driving to the church on the busy highway, Daphne glanced in her rearview mirror to find cars whizzing by as if she were standing still. She looked at her speedometer. She was going fifty, a perfectly rational speed for such a treacherous four-lane highway, even if the posted speed limit was fifty-five. A truck roared by, nearly forcing her car off the road. Daphne bit her lip and tried to still the rapid beating of her heart. If anything happened to her or the car, she would blame Rodney for this. His incessant plea that she attend this event had worn her down to the breaking point.

Another horn beeped at her from behind.

Hurry, hurry. These people never seem to show any respect for older people, she thought. Daphne gripped the steering wheel with both hands, ignoring the stares she received from other drivers.

Finally she made it to Rodney's church to see people gathering in the large yard for the Spring Fling. Tables and lawn chairs had been set up. Another banquet table, draped in a tablecloth that fluttered in the breeze, held an assortment of delectable homemade goodies. Daphne stepped out of her car to find Rodney greeting her with a huge smile on his face.

"I just knew you'd come," he said, taking the salad from her hands.

"This is the last time I do anything for you," she whispered but with a smile. It went without saying that Rodney was like a son to her. She looked upon this act as a small way of repaying him for his kindness and his excellent work at the nursery.

Rodney only laughed. "Miss Elliot, your heart is too big to think of something like that. Come on. I saved you a nice comfortable lawn chair."

She followed him to where members of the church had gathered. Rodney introduced her to everyone, along with comments about her wonderful nursery with the best assortment of plants this side of Charlottesville. Daphne felt slightly embarrassed by the way Rodney was gushing over her, but perhaps something could be gained from her willingness to eat with strangers out in the fresh air. If it brought more customers to the store, that was a good thing. She settled herself in a chair and watched young children zoom to and fro, playing with a ball. A woman came up and mentioned the beautiful rosebush she had purchased from the nursery last year and how she was looking forward to the gorgeous red blossoms. Daphne immediately perked up at this and offered her best smile.

"I'll be putting my roses on sale soon," she said. "You can save 20 percent."

"Well, then, I'll have to check it out. Thank you." The woman moved off to greet other church patrons. Daphne observed people roaming about, meeting each other, and conversing. She sighed, wishing she knew someone to talk to. Maybe it would have been better to invite a companion from her own church to tag along. At least she wouldn't feel so out of place.

She turned then in time to see a brown truck enter the parking lot. When she saw a familiar figure emerge from the driver's seat, dressed in a light blue shirt and jeans, her heart began to flutter.

Oh no! He couldn't have. But he did. Rodney had gone and invited Jack McNary to the affair. Of all the diabolical tricks. No wonder Rodney had been adamant that she come. Why he thought the two of them should get together anyway went beyond her sense of reasoning.

There was one way out of this, and that way was her car. She hurried off to the parking lot, only to find that another car had pulled in behind hers. She was blocked in with no place to go.

CHAPTER 4

"Miss Elliot, I'd like you to meet Jack Mc-Nary," Rodney said with a chuckle, taking her by the arm to lead her over to where the man was standing.

She wrestled her arm out of his grasp. "If I had a broom, I wouldn't hesitate to use it," she whispered.

"Look — you said strangers made you nervous. So I decided to invite a few people you did know."

That man isn't one of them. He killed all the plants he bought from the nursery. Daphne bit her tongue and glanced back to the white-frame church with the steeple that reached toward heaven, framed by the Blue Ridge Mountains. She would try to control her thoughts and her anxiety here on holy ground.

Jack McNary carried a foil-covered dish, which he placed on the table along with the other food. All at once, the pastor announced the blessing. Daphne bowed her head but kept it tipped to one side, watching Jack McNary out of the corner of her eye. He had removed his straw hat, bowed his head, and closed his eyes in a most reverent fashion. She wondered where he went to church.

With the blessing said, everyone hastened to form a line before the food. To Daphne's delight, the children shouted over the fruited gelatin salad, which was dished up by large spoonfuls. Jack came up to her, his plate already bursting with food, including a large helping of her salad. Daphne ignored him as she grabbed a paper plate and headed down the line.

"So how are you doing today, Miss Elliot?" Jack said.

Daphne realized it would be rude to ignore the man, even if he did destroy the plants from her nursery. What harm was there in being friendly, after all, especially at a church function? Daphne turned and nodded politely at him. "Just fine. A lovely day for a picnic." Her hand trembled as she tried to spoon up some baked beans.

"Can I help you with that?"

"No, thank you. I'm not quite ready for a nursing home."

The young girl behind her burst out

laughing. "You sound like my grandma. She's nearly ninety and still lives alone."

"Well, I hope I don't look that old," Daphne remarked. "I'm only sixty-five, but the doctor says my heart is eighty. I have to be careful."

"Then you'd better not eat any of the ham," Jack said, nodding at the ham arranged on a platter, surrounded by slices of juicy pineapple and maraschino cherries. "Too much salt."

Daphne felt her ire rise. She had been contemplating sneaking a piece of ham onto her plate. She bit back a retort with the girl still behind her and instead reached for a chicken leg. With her plate about half full, Daphne headed back for the lawn chair when she saw Rodney frantically waving his hand from a distant table.

"Right here, Miss Elliot. Melanie and I saved you a place."

Daphne managed a smile at everyone, reminding herself that each face was a potential customer for her nursery. She had just set down her plate when Jack came and occupied the seat directly opposite her. If things were not difficult enough, he had to sit right in front of her. And likely she would need an antacid after this meal with the way he was staring at her.

Inhaling a breath, Daphne decided to get the conversation off on the right foot. "Nice to see you again," she said to Melanie. "I've been keeping your husband out of trouble."

"I wish you would. Trouble is his specialty." A small smile quivered on the corner of her lips at the quip, but her eyes seemed to tell a different story. Daphne could tell much about people by the way their eyes radiated either happiness or sorrow. Looking back at Jack, she saw his eyes conveying an internal message, as well — like appreciation. Or was it something else?

Jack lifted a forkful of the fruited salad. "I hear you made this, Miss Elliot." He swallowed, then exclaimed, "Delicious!"

"Thank you." She picked up a chicken leg and began nibbling at it, her appetite all but gone with this uncomfortable scene unfolding at the table.

"And I hear you made this, Jack," Rodney added, pointing to the heap of barbecue on his plate.

Jack nodded. "I was telling Miss Elliot the other day that I make a mean barbecue. But I left out the hot pepper sauce, in case you wanted to try some, Miss Elliot."

She dared not refuse with everyone at the table staring at her expectantly. "All right, I will."

Rodney immediately jumped to his feet to bring her a plate of barbecue while Jack grinned from ear to ear. Inwardly she hoped he would not latch onto this as a cue that she was seeking a relationship. *I'm only doing it because the pastor and his wife have just sat down at the table and everyone is staring.*

Rodney returned with the plate, and she smiled at him until he gave her a thumbs-up signal. How she wanted to scold that young man for his wild ideas. He might mean well, but little did he know he was contributing to her heart condition. She had told him countless times that she loved her life as it was right now. She and Chubs were getting along just fine, even if she did feel a bit lonely at times. Why did he seem to think she needed a man to balance it all out?

Jack waited in anticipation for Daphne to take her first bite of his barbecue. She did so, only to discover it was quite good, despite herself. When he wasn't looking, she took several more bites until his gaze returned to her. The people around the table made small talk about a summer Bible study coming up and other activities of the church.

"So where do you go to church, Jack?" Rodney asked.

"I think I'm sold on this place, to be honest. I've been looking around for a good church family, and I think I've found it here."

"Great! Glad to have you. And what about you, Miss Elliot?" Rodney asked with a gleam in his eye. "Are you ready to make the switch?"

"You know perfectly well I'm quite happy where I am." Then she added hastily for the pastor's benefit, "Though this is a lovely church with wonderful people." She began feeling lightheaded. "Excuse me, but I think I'm going to have to call it a day."

"Not already," Rodney moaned. "You just got here."

"Really, I think I need to go home and rest. It's been a pretty exciting day."

"No more exciting than a full day in the nursery, I expect," Jack added.

Daphne gritted her teeth. He could see right through her, as if her very soul were transparent. Why was this happening to her now? "Thank you very much for inviting me."

"Aw, Miss Elliot. We were just going to start a croquet game. You need a little exercise to settle the stomach." Rodney pulled Melanie up by her hand.

"Please come and play, Miss Elliot," Melanie implored. "Then I won't feel lonely."

Daphne gazed into the face of the young woman before her. Melanie was a sweet thing with a heart of gold. She had made a beautiful bride a year ago. Rodney loved her very much, she could tell. The love they shared shone through Rodney's work at the nursery and perhaps even propelled him to try his hand at matchmaking, much to Daphne's chagrin. "I might play for a little bit."

Rodney whooped and cheered as if a football team had just scored a touchdown. His enthusiasm made Daphne all the more determined to see this picnic through to the end, even if Jack's company left her feeling uncomfortable. She refused to display emotion when Jack trailed behind and selected his own mallet, ready to join in the game. He picked red. Red had been Henry's favorite color whenever he played. Daphne's brother, Charles, introduced Henry to the game when he came visiting one summer. They all laughed and cheered as the ball rolled through the steel wickets. Even when Henry had the opportunity of sending Daphne's ball away after his ball hit hers, he never did. "If I sent you away, love, I would die," he said before throwing her a kiss that Daphne pretended to catch. It became a game, throwing kisses and catching them in the air. She often did it on the eve of his return to Tennessee, hoping he would not forget her, despite the distance.

Daphne shook her head, positioned herself at the starting pole, and hit her ball. It rolled cleanly through the two wickets.

"Good shot." Jack rested his mallet on one shoulder. "I can tell you've played this game before."

"Many times," Daphne said. She dearly wanted to expound on her croquet abilities and how she'd beat family members nearly every time. Instead, she swallowed her pride and whacked the ball, putting it in front of the next wicket. If only croquet had been introduced in the Summer Olympics, she often quipped. It was the only athletic-type event she excelled at, except perhaps for a marathon of repotting plants, of which the record stood at 110 in one day. Daphne smiled at her imagination as a ball went sailing past her feet toward the wicket. She jumped back with a slight yelp, only to see Jack racing toward her with a look of concern on his face.

"Did I hurt you, Daphne? Are you all right?"

She blinked, caught off guard by the tenderness of his words and the way he said her name. It was a sound she heard often in her dreams before they turned to nightmares. "I'm fine. The ball just startled me."

"You don't want to get hit by one of them."

"I should say not. I have been hit, and it nearly cost me my big toe." She blinked at his concern. It had been so long since any man of her age had shown concern for her well-being. If only she could be certain the concern was genuine and not born from some ulterior motive.

Just behind them, Melanie and Rodney were struggling with their mallets and balls, trying to overtake Jack and Daphne. Melanie hit her ball with a frustrated whack, sending it down a small incline away from the intended wicket. She tried to wear a smile, but Daphne could clearly see her aggravation. "It's just a game. Don't worry about it."

"I'll try not to," she said, then turned to see Rodney hit his ball with force, knocking it past the wicket and directly into Melanie's ball. "Aha!" he said with glee. "Revenge at last." He came and positioned the balls beside his foot.

"What are you going to do?" Melanie asked.

"If you hit a player's ball, you have the

choice of taking two hits or sending the opponent's ball away and using one hit."

"Why don't you take the two hits?" Jack suggested. "It would put you in the lead."

An impish spark lit his face. "This is more fun."

Rodney raised the mallet and let it go with a smash, sending Melanie's ball careening past the field of play and over to where some of the picnickers were sitting at a table eating dessert.

"Thanks a lot," Melanie mumbled. "I should be the one sending you away after you didn't pay the electric bill."

Rodney's face reddened. "You don't have to tell the world about that, Melanie."

"Why not? You were the one who left me in the dark and without hot water for my shower." She turned to Jack and Daphne. "Here I was, in the middle of my shower, when the electricity goes off! I thought someone had hit a pole. I called the electric company. Come to find out, Rod hadn't paid the electric bill."

"It was an oversight," he declared, twirling the mallet around, his cheerful disposition slowly changing like a freshly peeled apple turning brown. "And I said you didn't need to go tell the world about our business."

"Let's not worry about it," Jack said. "I know I've made plenty of mistakes, too." He gave a sideways glance toward Daphne. She wondered if he was still trying to apologize for destroying the precious plants she'd sold him.

From that moment on, the game took a turn for the worse. Melanie and Rodney hardly spoke to each other while the balls trickled through the wickets and onward toward home base. Daphne found the joy in the game wane under the blanket of competitiveness. It reminded her of her brother, Charles, when she used to play games with him. He had to win over her in every game, as if to show off his dominion as the older brother. If she dared win, he would sulk for a week.

When Daphne continued to play well, cruising in to win the croquet game, she half expected Jack to throw a fit. Instead he smiled and congratulated her on her win. "I'm going to have to brush up on my skills if I ever hope to beat you," he commented.

"I don't see why. When do we ever plan to play again?"

"You have a nice lawn by your home. We could set up a course over there sometime and play."

Daphne stared at him in horror. "How do

you know where I live?"

Jack paled and looked away.

"You've been snooping around, haven't you? Well, I won't have it. Please just leave me alone." She began striding toward her car.

"Daphne, I mean, Miss Elliot, wait now. I wasn't snooping. I did notice the other day after work when you drove home. It's not like your house is hidden. It's only a mile from the nursery."

"It doesn't matter. You shouldn't be prying into other people's affairs —" She stopped when she heard arguing near her car. She looked about, only to find Rodney and Melanie shouting at each other. Melanie was holding a tissue and dabbing her eyes.

"I don't care if it was embarrassing to you. You embarrass me, living as we do, wondering how we're going to survive. And I want a baby. How can we have a baby with no money? You said I wouldn't have to go back to that awful office, and now it looks as if I'll have to."

"Melanie, it isn't that bad."

"It is bad! When we can't even pay the electric bill, that's bad. And how are we going to pay the other debts?"

Rodney looked up and saw Daphne standing there. No doubt she must've had a strange expression on her face, for he shook his head and strode back to the picnic. Daphne wanted to say something but didn't know what. Instead, Melanie took off in the opposite direction, to a bank of trees away from everyone else. *It's so hard to see young ones quarrel,* she thought.

All at once she saw herself and Henry standing by a bank of trees, with a raging river flowing before them. Henry was holding his favorite fishing pole.

"But you said we could take a walk!"

"We will, to my favorite fishing hole. Really, Daphne, the weather is wonderful, perfect for fishing."

"You mean perfect for doing what you want to do. What about me? I came here to visit you, and you'd rather go fishing."

"Daphne, it makes no difference whether it's a walk or casting a line into the river, as long as we're together."

"It makes a lot of difference."

She could picture the two of them bantering back and forth until a deep voice said, "They sound just like us."

The voice sent shivers racing through her, until she found Jack glancing down at her. He pointed at the young couple who had meandered off to separate locations.

"I don't know what you mean."

"You know, what happened between us just now and even back at the nursery when I told you about my plants. In fact, at the nursery you acted as if I had killed your relatives."

"The plants are my relatives. I have no one else on this earth. I'm all alone."

"Daphne, you aren't alone any longer. You may think you're alone, but there is someone who . . ."

Daphne searched through her pockets for the keys. Obviously the man thought he was the perfect person to ease her loneliness. Maybe he was, but at that moment, she couldn't accept it. "Excuse me, but I need to go home. Chubs needs a walk, and I need to rest."

"Daphne, if I said anything to —"

"Never mind. I just want to tell you that, yes, I am alone in this world. There is no one else. And it's all right. I'm content to be that way." She headed for the car without looking back to see his reaction. She was thankful the vehicle that had blocked her in was gone. Once in the driver's seat, she saw Jack walk up to several people and offer his hand. He was easy around strangers, giving them a smile and words of encouragement. Why did she have to be so short with him?

"Because I can't take any more pain in my life," she said aloud. She didn't want to admit that Jack had stirred something within her. It seemed to ease the bitterness that had held her heart captive for so long. If only she would let go completely and embrace the future. Perhaps Rodney was right. Perhaps the reason her heart ached so much was because she never did cast the disappointment into the Lord's capable hands.

Daphne shook her head. The whole picnic had been a fiasco, as she'd known it would be. Why had she ever agreed to go? And, to top it all, Rodney and Melanie were fighting. They were a picture of love, a symbol of what she and Henry might have been. The idea of their lashing out at each other sent waves of consternation flowing through Daphne. She prayed they would reconcile, and soon.

CHAPTER 5

Daphne considered playing the love song from *Bambi* over a small stereo she kept in the back room if she thought it would help Rodney's mood. Since the day of the picnic, the young man had brooded. He never smiled, nor did his beautiful tenor voice bellow out a favorite song. Daphne was amazed at how much his singing had become a part of her establishment. The silence brought emptiness to the place. If only she knew what to say or do. Daphne had to admit that personal relationships were not her strong point. Her brother had often said that a rabid dog would get along better with her than anyone. That's what made her relationship with Henry so special. They were meant to be together. He helped soften her rough edges, like a chisel to a piece of stone. He coaxed her along and showed her mercy, softening her hard heart.

Daphne stood outside the nursery as a

large truck pulled in, transporting the plants and shrubs she had ordered for the early summer season. Two men jumped out and greeted her enthusiastically.

"Got any cookies today, Miss Elliot?" one of them asked.

"Sorry, fellows. I bake cookies only once a year," she said, referring to the large platter of oatmeal raisin cookies she had baked in February. When the men had arrived back then with her spring plants, they'd gobbled down the cookies faster than a pack of wild dogs.

"Too bad. Guess we need to work harder for the goodies." The men huffed, unloading box after box of plants, which Daphne directed them to place on several long wooden tables.

As they worked, she searched the road for Rodney. It was unusual for him to be late. She had counted on his being there to direct the men with the plants. She was thankful the men were easygoing and took to calling her their mom. The cheerful flowers waving in the brisk breeze sent warmth flowing through her. She looked over the flats and nodded. They included impatiens of different colors, begonias, and vinca, not to mention the vegetable flats of peppers, tomatoes, squashes, and herbs. They were all her babies in need of a good home.

Next came a new supply of rosebushes that looked like thorny twigs sticking out of their pots. With a little water, sunshine, and tender loving care, the roses would put forth leaves and then shoots of flowery heads with a fragrance that filled the air.

"So where's Rodney?" asked one of the men.

"I don't know. He's been having some problems. I hope that has nothing to do with his being late."

"Too bad. Hope it's nothing serious. That man seems so happy about everything."

Daphne agreed, realizing how Rodney's joyful outlook on life lifted her spirits. Seeing him like this, caught in the midst of some marital conflict, burdened her to no end.

"I'm sure you can help him, Miss Elliot. He thinks real highly of you. He told us so."

The comment pleased her, but she shook her head. "That young man has a mind of his own, unfortunately." She took the shipping slip the man gave her and wished him a pleasant day. Gazing about the area, she noticed the large bags of mulch and fertilizer that still needed to be stacked. Where could Rodney be?

The roar of an engine sent her whirling

about, only to see a familiar dirt brown truck pull into the parking lot. The lone occupant wore a straw hat. She nearly groaned out loud but instead looked at the bags and how they made her nursery appear unkempt.

"You look like something's on your mind, Miss Elliot," Jack McNary observed, striding toward her.

"I don't know what to do. My employee isn't here this morning. He didn't call to tell me he wouldn't be in. I have all those bags that need stacking."

Jack lifted his straw hat and scratched his head. "I'll be glad to stack them for you."

"I can't pay you," she said quickly. "I have this huge shipping bill to pay and —"

"I didn't say you had to pay me. A smile would be enough." He strode over to the bags. "Where do you want them?"

Daphne gaped at him before pointing to the area. Jack hefted the bags one by one and set them in their proper place. His strength amazed her. Even Rodney grunted and groaned under the weight of the bags he was forced to bear. This man slung the sacks around as if they were filled with downy feathers.

"I guess you're used to carrying heavy loads," Daphne observed.

"Sure am. Worked on a farm for a few years. I got used to lugging feed bags and hay bales. This is nothing, really."

Daphne nearly cried with his willingness to help her out of her predicament, despite her rudeness the day of the picnic. At times she felt the Lord working on her heart, giving her the gift of repentance, but the flesh kept her silent. At last she turned and told him how delicious his barbecue was at the picnic and how she was sorry things didn't turn out better between them. He gazed back at her, somewhat amazed by her response. The look made her blink twice. It was a familiar look to her, a look of tenderness she couldn't quite place. Maybe it was just a longing within her to have a man gaze at her in such a fashion, even if her mind was telling her not to get involved.

Embarrassed by it all, Daphne hastily retreated to the store to take inventory of the summer stock. Every so often she glanced over to make sure Jack was stacking the bags correctly. She decided she must give him something for his labor. She would offer him several bags of mulch in exchange for his help. A meal would be more in keeping, as her father used to pay men for their labor by having Mother feed them a home-cooked dinner, like meat loaf and potatoes.

But the idea of Jack eating at her home made her stomach lurch.

"All set," he said with a grin. "Now what did I come here for? I can't remember."

"Mulch," she said. "That is, you can take several bags of mulch."

"Mulch? What do I need mulch for?"

"I'm paying you with mulch. You need mulch with the kind of summers we get here in Virginia. It will keep the plants from drying out. Take several bags."

"Then I guess I'd better have some, since I already know what dry plants mean." Jack lifted up several bags of mulch and placed them in the bed of his truck. "Thank you very much, Miss Elliot."

"I should be thanking you. I needed the help. Now I'm going to call that young man and find out what happened to him."

"If you need any more help, let me know. In fact, I'll give you my phone number, in case."

Daphne's face colored at the thought. "That's all right. I don't need —"

He ignored her and fetched a crumbled piece of paper from the front pocket of his overalls, along with the stub of a pencil. He scrawled out the phone number and the name, along with his address. "Here you go. For a rainy day."

Daphne took the piece of paper and immediately stuffed it into the pocket of her apron. She said a quick good-bye to him as he trudged off to his truck. God had brought Jack McNary here when she needed him. She couldn't deny it. After the truck left, she reached inside her apron pocket and withdrew the slip of paper. The letters were short and choppy. She noted that he lived on Spring Mountain Road. She knew where that was, right beside the mountains. Rodney always said he wanted a place one day by the mountains. The thought reminded her of her employee's unexplained tardiness.

She entered the store, left the note on the back counter, and went at once to call Rodney. The phone rang incessantly until an answering machine picked up. After leaving a brief message, she hung up with a sigh. *Rodney, please don't do this to me. Dear God, what am I going to do?*

"Where were you yesterday?"

Rodney looked at her in surprise. He came that morning on time, to Daphne's relief, yet with a strange air about him.

"Didn't Melanie call?"

"No."

"Figures. I knew she wouldn't." He

banged the counter with his fist, an uncharacteristic gesture for him, before striding to the back where he deposited his lunch and a magazine. "I told her to call you and let you know I wouldn't be in."

"I never got a call. Yesterday was the summer delivery, too. I'm glad Jack, I mean, Mr. McNary, showed up when he did. He helped stack the mulch and the fertilizer."

"It wasn't my fault, Miss Elliot. I left instructions for her to call, but she does what she pleases these days. And now I'm in hot water with you. Just my luck."

Daphne didn't know what to think. Never had she seen Rodney so irate. It made her wish for the old days and his songs of love infiltrating the place, even if the singing rubbed her nerves the wrong way. "Now don't fret. Things will get better with Melanie."

"Fat chance," he mumbled. "We haven't had a decent conversation since the day of the picnic. I'm sorry I asked you to go. I had no business trying to set you up with anyone. Believe me, you're better off not being married, Miss Elliot. No wonder God says it's better for a man to live on a roof than to be in the same house with a contentious woman."

Daphne began sorting out seed packets,

finding some outdated packets still on the store shelves that Rodney was supposed to purge last fall. "Have you found out why Melanie is so upset?"

"It's this job."

Daphne whirled to face him. Any mention of her business, whether good or bad, piqued her interest. Not that she wanted to hear anything bad about the way she ran things. Oh, there was the occasional customer who said that a plant she'd sold them was diseased, or the customer who found a hole in a bag of potting mix. She did everything she could to fix the problem. "What did she say?"

"It doesn't matter." He disappeared into the storeroom.

Daphne could hardly contain her curiosity. Of course discussions should remain private between couples, but if the argument had anything do with her business, she must know what was going on. Did Melanie think she was treating Rodney unfairly? She only kept him beyond closing time one day a week at most. He didn't seem to mind. The spring was extra busy, after all. Or perhaps she expected Daphne to pay him more? But Daphne did pay him far more than other employees she had had under her care. And what about her idea of giving Rodney the business? How could she do that if Melanie disapproved of his job?

Tossing the outdated seed packets into the garbage, Daphne went to the greenhouse where she found Rodney with his feet buried in dirt. He had upset a bag of soil kept on the shelf, the potting mixture Daphne used for transplanting her most prized plants. "Now I know something is wrong," she observed.

Rodney tried to scoop it up with his sneaker.

"A broom and a dustpan are probably better." She picked up a broom and began sweeping.

Rodney took the implement out of her hands. "I'll do it. This is my life right now. One big pile of dirt."

"It can't be that bad. Surely Melanie isn't still upset about your sending her croquet ball away on Sunday."

Rodney chuckled. "If only it were that." He leaned against the handle of the broom. "Miss Elliot, I'm afraid I'm going to have to move on to other pastures."

"What?"

"Melanie says we don't have any money. I told her when we got married she could stop with her office work and concentrate on her silk flower business. She wants to do those craft shows, you know. She couldn't stand the office. It was like a cage, and the boss was a dictator."

"I remember, I think."

"Well, she's mad the electric bill didn't get paid last month, and she's been complaining about the money ever since. She said I lied about my income and that I didn't make enough here to feed a flea. And what are we supposed to do if a baby comes along? Et cetera."

Daphne could feel the heat rise in her cheeks. "You make much more than any other employee I've had."

"She's not happy. So I'm going to have to look for another job."

He maneuvered the broom, sweeping the dirt into a pile. Daphne picked up the dustpan and gingerly knelt while Rodney swept. In the dustpan, she saw all her dreams ready to be thrown into the garbage. *Dear God, this can't be happening.*

"I know this must make you real upset, Miss Elliot," he said with a chuckle. "It means you won't have to hear any more of my singing or witness my numerous schemes in life."

I would take all of that and more. He simply can't leave! What will I do? She felt her chest tighten and her heart begin to race. She turned from him and made her way to the counter where she sat down in a chair.

"Are you all right?" Rodney asked.

"You can't do this to me. Please."

"Miss Elliot, I don't have a choice."

"There are always choices. I will go over the books tonight. I'll see if I can give you a raise."

Rodney rested the broom against the wall and came to her. His rugged face softened into the tender look of a son for his mother, so much so that Daphne nearly cried. "I won't let you do that. You'll be eating dog food for dinner if you give me any more money."

"If I lose you, I'll have to sell."

"No, you won't. You'll find another helper. I'll ask around church. I know some guys who would jump at the chance for a good job like this."

Daphne shook her head. She couldn't stand the thought of a major change in her life, especially training a new person. Everything right now was at a status quo, organized, in a daily routine. One change and she might slide down some slippery slope toward disaster. She had been through too many changes already in her life. She couldn't lose the young man who had helped her so much. Rodney gave her place of business character. He was helpful to the customers. And, yes, she treasured his songs of love, even if she was slow to acknowledge it.

"Miss Elliot, I must tell you the truth. If it comes down to my marriage or this job, you know what I have to do."

Daphne twisted her hands in dismay. She knew very well what he was saying. It was his character, after all. Rodney loved Melanie, and he loved being married, even if they were having difficulties right now. She couldn't expect him to be married to a job. That's what wrecked relationships and sent marriages tumbling into a dark abyss. "I know," she said quietly, though the words felt forced.

The rest of the day was somber, matching the dark gray clouds that began drifting across the spring sky. When Daphne closed the doors of the nursery that evening, she wondered how long the business would stay afloat now that Rodney had all but resigned. She hurried to the car, thankful she lived only a mile away as raindrops began falling from above.

She negotiated the short drive home, and pulling in, she heard Chubs barking. Lightning flashed. A violent spring storm was brewing. Virginia was known to have storms like this with flooding rain and even hail. Daphne hurried into the home as lightning struck again, followed by a boom of thunder that rattled the windows in their frames.

Chubs began to howl and scurried upstairs to hide under the bed, even though he desperately needed to go outdoors. Daphne managed to coax him out with a dog biscuit, hooked the leash on his collar, and allowed him to step outside the back door to do his business. The rain came down in a torrent. Chubs was soaked almost immediately, forcing Daphne to keep him in the kitchen lest he shake water all over the carpet in the living room. Muddy paw prints added a new decoration to the flowery print of the linoleum floor. Daphne watched the lightning dance across the sky. A bolt zipped between her home and the nursery. The indoor lights flickered. Despite his wet fur, Daphne hugged Chubs, thankful for the dog's companionship on this stormy evening. What a terrible day it had been, with Rodney's surprise announcement and now a storm that left her feeling weak and lonely.

She went to the living room and plopped down in her favorite chair. The rain outside continued in earnest, no doubt washing away the new soil she had put in her home garden not too long ago. She wondered if

Jack had put down the mulch before the storm hit. She slid back in the chair, listening to the sound of the rain splattering against the windows. If only someone were here to share her innermost thoughts and, yes, her fears, too.

All at once she saw herself and Henry ducking between raindrops during a walk in the woods. She had thought to bring an umbrella, and together they snuggled under it while sitting on a small log just big enough for the two of them. The fragrance of the woods was even more pronounced. She shivered a bit before feeling the warmth of his arm cradled about her.

"Cold?"

"A little." Her voice quivered.

He removed his coat and placed it around her shoulders. Soon they were sharing a kiss beneath the umbrella. It didn't matter that the rain had begun to drip off the umbrella and fall into her lap. She only basked in Henry's warm presence and his lips that made her forget all her worries in life. Love could do that to you. Anxieties melted away under its fire. Problems were dissolved. Trials were but dust specks in the wind.

Daphne straightened in her seat. Melanie and Rodney had love, and that's what would see them through this difficulty. They needed to be like her and Henry, full of love for each other, even if they were caught in a storm with rain drenching them.

Daphne grabbed the telephone to call them.

"Are you all right, Miss Elliot?" Rodney asked when he answered.

"Yes, but I know you two are not. So I'd like to invite myself over to your place for dinner. Ask your lovely wife if I can come."

"Of course you can come. But I'm warning you, if you think it will change anything —"

"I'm just lonely here, especially with this storm. I want to eat with someone tomorrow night." She heard conversation in the background and Melanie quickly agreeing to a guest for dinner.

"Of course you're welcome to come over."

"Will I see you tomorrow for work?"

"I'm not leaving yet."

"Good. See you tomorrow." Daphne replaced the receiver with a decisive click. She refused to let this relationship go to ruin, and likewise her business. She would coax them along on that sailboat of love and make certain it brought them into a safe harbor. If not, she had no idea where the storm might end up sending her and the garden center.

CHAPTER 6

Daphne tried to maintain an air of business at the nursery the following day, but she couldn't help her anxiety over the dinner that night. Rodney stayed busy outside, assisting customers with bags of fertilizer, mulch, and soil while she worked the cash register. Business had picked up with the spring planting season in full swing. The mere idea that Rodney might walk out on her during the busiest time of the year made her insides ache. By the time she trained another person to take his place, she would lose much of the season. And if a season went bad, she would have no choice but to close.

On her lunch break, she considered her options while trying to eat a dry turkey sandwich. Like other upsetting days, she found her appetite greatly diminished. Not that she couldn't stand to shed a few pounds, but anxiety was not the way to lose weight. As her doctor once told her, a diet low in salt and cholesterol, along with a brief walk, would help.

For now, Daphne put all that aside to concentrate on her dilemma. For some reason, she thought of Jack and his willingness to help her stack the soil and mulch after the delivery. Just as quickly, she shook her head. She couldn't possibly have that man fill Rodney's shoes. He was too old, for one thing. What if he died of a heart attack, trying to lift all those bags? And she couldn't boss him around the way she could Rodney. No, it would have to be someone young and with an openness to tolerate her way of doing things, like Rodney.

Daphne bit her lip and put down her half-eaten sandwich. Life was getting far too complicated. She had endured years of pain and uncertainty. At this point in her life she was growing weary of it all. Perhaps it would be better if her heart did give out so she could be at home with the Lord. But she wasn't a quitter. She was an Elliot and carried her namesake with pride. Her father had begun this business, and she would do whatever she could to keep it alive.

Before going to the dinner, Daphne outfitted herself in a pantsuit and the pearl earrings. She liked to wear them when times were rough. It made her remember all that she had been through with God's help. Daphne paused, her hand frozen with the lipstick ready to trace color on her dry lips. *God's help.* The very words convicted her. Had she truly been relying on God's help through all this? Or had she been trying to do it in her own strength, fueled only by pride? She applied the color, then used a tissue to wipe away the tiny streaks that missed her lips. She didn't want to miss God in all this. He had been there for her in the past and would guide her future if she allowed Him.

Daphne went to the chair in the living room and sat down. She closed her eyes and offered a prayer for help that God would guide her. Above all, she prayed that He would lead her to make the right decision with regard to her business. When she snapped open her eyes, the light of the lamp seemed to shine a little brighter. Her heart beat stronger. She smiled and picked up her purse. God was still there.

Daphne admired the many silk flower arrangements Melanie had created. The spare bedroom was filled with all kinds of arrangement paraphernalia — dried flowers, baskets, ribbon, picks. The strange aromas made her sneeze.

"These are wonderful," she said, picking up a small basket. "How much do you want for it?"

Melanie gazed at her in surprise. "If you want it, go ahead and take it."

"Nonsense. A worker is worthy of wages." Daphne opened her purse. "Is twenty enough?"

Melanie smiled and accepted the bill. She began wrapping plastic around the arrangement while Daphne examined the other arrangements sitting on a card table. "Have you done any craft shows?"

"A few. I've been trying to get that craft store in town to sell some of them on consignment. Of course I'm in competition with everyone else." She sighed. "But the way things are going right now, I may have to get rid of the business anyway and look for a job."

Daphne inhaled a breath. The door had opened already. She prayed she had the strength to handle whatever walked through. "So things are a little tight?"

Melanie chuckled. "*Tight* is hardly the word I would use. *Impossible* is more like it. I know you're very generous with your salary to Rod, Miss Elliot, but right now we're having trouble paying the bills. Not that it helps when he forgets to make payments on time and then we end up having to pay late fees. The bank had to pay on two checks because we didn't have enough funds to cover them. That's sixty dollars in service charges. It's a waste."

"Now we all make mistakes —" Daphne stopped when she saw the lines of consternation creep across the young woman's face. "I mean, I miss bills." She fingered a silk flower arrangement in a basket shaped like an old-fashioned baby buggy.

"I know I'll have to go back to that terrible office again. Rod promised me I wouldn't. He said I could do my flower business. Now I don't think he cares."

Daphne saw the shadow of Rodney on the back patio, using a small grill to barbecue chicken. At times the hazy smoke obscured him from view. She felt more and more like a concerned parent, trying to dole out advice to these two young people.

"He used to care. But I really think he does want me to go back to work. He says that most home businesses fail after a year anyway. Since I haven't had any major contracts for this work, he thinks it's a failure."

"A businesswoman can succeed," Daphne said with a smile, sparking one on Melanie's face. "I'm living proof. It isn't easy, but with God, all things are possible."

"Yes, but there's so much pressure for women to make it big in the corporate world. I feel as if I'm a failure because I want to run a home business and stay at home with any kids we might have."

"There's nothing wrong with a home business. And don't you listen to any of that chatter you hear on television. You have a very important role here, too. I do think you need to advertise your work more. It's really beautiful."

"Advertising costs money."

Just then the phone rang. Melanie picked it up, then marched away to give the receiver to Rodney. While she was gone, Daphne took stock of Melanie's inventory. She wondered if perhaps some of the customers at her nursery would want a few artificial arrangements for their homes. The thought made her cringe. If they bought them, they would never come and buy real plants and planting material for gardens. She shook her head, unwilling to make that kind of commitment yet.

Melanie returned. "Dinner's almost ready, Miss Elliot."

Daphne followed the young woman to the small kitchen nook. She saw the old flowered furniture in the tiny living room, given to Melanie when her grandmother passed on. The room was fairly bursting with furniture of various shapes and sizes. She could see right there that they needed a bigger place.

Daphne looked up to see Rodney emerge from the patio, carrying a platter of chicken and wearing a grin on his face. "I've cured all our ills," he announced, placing the platter on the table.

Melanie stared at him quizzically while Daphne exclaimed how delicious the food looked.

"We'll pray. Then I'll tell you my news," Rodney said with a grin.

The three bowed their heads while he offered up a prayer for the meal.

Daphne accepted a bowl of seasoned rice. "So what's the news?"

"You probably won't like it much, Miss Elliot, but I have great news. I'm set for an interview tomorrow with the company I e-mailed a resume to just yesterday. Isn't that terrific?"

Daphne stared. Before she knew what was happening, her hand trembled, spilling rice on the tablecloth. "Oh no."

"No harm done," Melanie said, grabbing a sponge to clean up the mess.

"If I get it, the job will pay big-time."

Daphne looked down at her food and found her appetite gone. Here she had come, hoping to solve this couple's problems, only to find more looming. What was she doing here then? Occupying a chair? She picked up her water glass and took a sip. "What does it pay?"

"Quite a bit. It starts at thirty-five with opportunities for more."

Daphne choked on the rice she had started eating. She picked up a napkin and coughed loudly. Rodney was only making twenty-eight in her little establishment. Her heart began to sink. She glanced over, expecting Melanie to smile at this announcement. Instead, she took only tiny bites of her food.

"It will work this time," Rodney told her.

"Right. I've heard it before, Rod. You go to these interviews, and then they make you sit by the phone for months. What happens to us in the meantime?"

Rodney glanced over at Daphne. No doubt he was hoping she would keep him on until he secured another job. Daphne bristled at the thought. If he was so eager to find a job paying thirty-five thousand dollars, why should she help? He would only leave anyway. She shook her head at such hardheartedness. Rodney was the best thing that had ever happened to her business. She could never let him go.

"In the meantime, I'll keep working."

"And in the meantime, we get more and more in debt," Melanie said with a groan. "We don't even have enough to make the car payment. I took out an ad today."

Rodney put down his fork. "What?"

"We can't afford the car, so I took out an ad to sell it."

Rodney rose to his feet, his face reddening. "Are you kidding? You're selling our car right out from underneath us?"

"We can't afford two cars. It's either that or we starve."

"Melanie, get real."

"No, you get real. And you haven't gotten real in the last six months. I got another notice about an overdue bill, too. The next thing we know, the electricity will be turned off again."

Daphne put down her fork. She felt dizzy and nauseated. The bickering weighed her down nearly to the breaking point. It seemed like a rerun from long ago. Finally she lifted her head and said, "That's enough. You two are hissing and barking like a cat and a dog. Next thing, you'll be scratching each other's eyes out."

Rodney sat down, and both he and Melanie bowed their heads, as if ashamed by their lack of self-control.

"I know what it's like not to have money. When my father died, there was a huge debt owed on the business. My brother, Charles, and I got into a terrible fight about it. He wanted to sell the business to pay off the debt. I wanted to keep it going and asked him to help. It was awful. We didn't speak. He left and went to live in California. I haven't seen him since. Is that what you want? Letting your marriage break up over this and living on opposite sides of the country?"

"It's not that bad," Rodney began, though his voice betrayed his doubt.

"Young man, I've seen many fine marriages break up over money. Yes, we need it to live, but money can end up breaking us and destroying everything we hold dear. That's when I made a decision long ago not to let money rule my life. I decided to live simply. I didn't buy fancy clothes. My furniture belonged to my parents. I bought a used car. And if I'm to have anything new, I'll leave it to God to bless me. And He has, I must say."

"I don't see anything wrong with wanting to buy a few new things," Melanie said in defense.

"Or having a car," Rodney added with a sideways glance at Melanie.

"Of course not. But, like everything in our lives, there's a right time for those things. Do you have a Bible?"

Rodney sat up, a bit startled. "Of course." He went to retrieve a Bible from the living room.

Daphne flipped it open. "Here it is. This is the verse God gave me when I was in debt. 'And my God will meet all your needs according to his glorious riches in Christ Jesus.' "

"So what you're saying is, we need to trust God in this," Rodney said, glancing toward Melanie.

"Yes. He knows what's best, and He knows our needs." Daphne realized she also needed to trust God more. Even as she spoke, the words convicted her own spirit. "Without faith, we can't please God. He wants us to trust Him, especially with our needs. He cares for the sparrow, and He makes the plants beautiful. Surely He will help us."

Melanie played with her napkin, folding and unfolding it. Daphne could see that the words were hard to accept. How she wanted to give these two young people a hug and tell them God would help, as He once helped her. He had answered her heartfelt cries when debts nearly forced her to declare bankruptcy and she had barely enough stock on the shelves to keep the nursery afloat. But somehow He had brought her through it. Now the business had a promising future — that is, if Rodney would stay on.

"I want my business to continue," she declared suddenly. "I don't want it to die when I do." She opened her purse and fished out a paper, one she had written the previous night by the light of a small oil lamp while the storm raged outside. She gave it to Rodney.

He took it and read it slowly, then flung the paper down. "Miss Elliot!"

"What is it?" Melanie asked.

Rodney gave her the paper. Daphne saw Melanie's cheeks pink and her lips tremble. "I don't believe it. You're giving the nursery business to Rod when you retire?"

"Yes, if he wants it. I had made the decision awhile ago, but I wasn't sure when would be the appropriate time to bring it up. Now seems a better time than any. If you agree, I'll have my lawyer make out an official document."

"I don't know what to say," Rodney began.

"You can say plenty. First of all, you can

tell your pretty wife here that you love her. Same with you, Melanie."

Rodney and Melanie stared at each other. Suddenly they broke out into laugher that played like a soothing melody after the disharmony witnessed earlier that night. "I do love you, Melanie," he said. "And with God's help, we're going to make it."

"I love you, too, Rod. And if I need to work for a time, it's okay. We'll do what we need to do."

He glanced back at the paper. "I really appreciate this, Miss Elliot, but are you sure you want to do this? Do you know who you're getting?"

"Yes, I know. I know for a fact that you remind me of Henry. He worked hard and did what he could with the job he had. And he loved to help others. I think of this as a memorial to his name."

Melanie took Daphne's hand and squeezed it. "You still miss him after all these years?"

Daphne couldn't help the tear that slipped out of her eye as she nodded. She hadn't anticipated such a reaction, but Melanie had touched a sensitive area.

"You never did tell me what happened," Rodney said.

"What? I'm sure I did." When he shook

his head, Daphne obliged. She wanted to relate the story, even if it was painful. She told about the day of his death and the mysterious fire at the mill that killed him.

"They were never able to tell you how it happened?"

"No. I went there myself and asked questions. No one would say. They just said it was a terrible accident. They said there was nothing left . . . only ashes." The tears gathered in her eyes. "I'm sorry." She blew her nose into the tissue Melanie had handed her. "I had a funeral for him, in my own way. I gave him to God. But that lumber mill stole him away."

"I wish I had known all this," Rodney said softly. "I know you mentioned Henry a few times and that he was your boyfriend when you were young, but I had no idea he died so tragically."

Melanie again gripped her hand. "Miss Elliot, I'm sure God doesn't want you to be alone like this. He will bring another man into your life. It's not too late to experience love."

The mere mention of another man instantly dried her tears and raised her defense mechanism like a solid wall. "No. My time is long gone, I'm afraid. The Lord is my husband. Scripture even says so."

Melanie released her hand and rose to clear the table. Rodney jumped up, as well, and before long had brewed Daphne a cup of tea. At first she regretted confessing her hurt over Henry's passing. Now, with her heart open and exposed, she realized the lingering sorrow that had crippled her. She had hoped to bring healing to this young couple but realized she needed some, as well.

CHAPTER 7

Daphne went to work feeling better than she had in months. Since giving the document to Rodney and Melanie and informing them of her desire to bequeath them the store once she retired, a heavy burden had been lifted from her shoulders. No longer would she lie awake nights, wondering what would become of her father's business if the Lord took her in her sleep. She could rest knowing that Rodney and Melanie would do a good job and keep the business thriving. Not only that, but she felt a renewal in her spiritual life, as well. For so long, she had shut out God. Sharing with the young couple from the Bible renewed her own interest in studying the Word and making it a greater part of her life. She read the Bible at breakfast over a bowl of bran cereal that morning and played a cassette tape of favorite hymns while she did a few chores.

Daphne worked with Rodney, arranging

the roses for the new sale they had just begun. He returned to singing his love songs, which was cheerful music to her ears. He talked incessantly of what he would like to do with the business, including incorporating Melanie's talent for flower arranging. "I hope you don't mind my talking about this," he said suddenly. "I mean, it's not as if I want you to retire anytime soon. I guess I'm just excited about being a business owner."

"Don't worry about me. I have a feeling that retirement may be just around the corner. It's good to hear a motivated young man toying with new ideas. Now let's put all the red roses together, right by the entrance to the nursery."

"Red is the color of love, Miss Elliot," Rodney said with a mischievous lilt to his voice.

"Yes, and if my mother were alive, she would surely appreciate a lovely red rose on Mother's Day, which is coming soon."

Rodney frowned. "You know what I mean. Don't try to change my words. And speaking of love . . ."

A familiar truck rolled slowly into the gravel parking lot of the nursery. Daphne stood fast in place, her head high, and even wore a smile on her lips. She would not let anything or anyone steal her joy this day, despite Rodney's connotations.

"Hello, Jack," Rodney said with a cheerful wave. "Have we got a wonderful rose for you!"

Daphne felt her face color like the red roses blooming in the pots. "Rodney, please take these shipping papers to my office."

"Sure, Miss Elliot. I can take a hint."

The heat in her face crept into her ears and down her neck. And she was wearing a light-colored top, too. No doubt she looked like a tomato dressed in white. *The nerve of him,* she thought, even as Rodney strode off whistling. Daphne stooped down, trying to rearrange the potted plants into straight rows. She murmured a greeting to Jack's pleasant "Good morning." So much for her plan to be friendly. Rodney had again succeeded in putting her in a less-than-pleasant mood.

"You've got some nice roses there," he observed. "I used to have a climbing rose by the front porch until it pretty near died on me." He paused and stepped back. "I shouldn't be telling you about dead plants. It isn't as if I killed it, though. It broke clean away after an ice storm during the winter. And then the beetles came and ate it."

"Roses are like children. They need tender, loving care."

"And I'm sure you know just what they need."

Daphne glanced up at him. No doubt he must be referring to her vast knowledge of plants. She couldn't see his expression through the shadow made by the straw hat, but she could imagine what he looked like — with blue eyes staring down and a funny smirk on his face. "I know a few things. I've been in this business long enough."

"I see that young fellow decided to come back. I thought maybe you might have lost him. That's why I came to find out if you needed any help."

"No. As you can see, he's back and quite happy about it."

"Also, I wanted to let you know that the new plants are doing just fine."

"Glad to hear it."

"So there's hope for me as a gardener?"

Daphne refused to go that far but managed to bite her tongue before telling him so.

"Anyway, I was wondering if you might still need an extra hand?"

Daphne stared back, ready to issue a firm retort.

"I work cheap," he added.

"But I have Rodney."

He exhaled a sigh as if disappointed over the fact. "As I said, I wasn't sure if he would be coming back. I mean, it isn't as if I need the money or anything. It's just —"

Daphne didn't want to hear what he was about to say. The mere thought that he might want to spend time with her made her anxious. Soon he would be asking her to go with him to a lecture at the senior center or invite her to the famous Hardware Store Restaurant downtown. Her knees began to quake at the thought of sitting in a restaurant with a flickering candle on the table, staring at another man. The last time she had sat at a table like that was with that sweet-talking Larson McCall, and she almost lost her business because of it.

She picked up a rosebush and began walking toward the store, thinking a bush by the entrance might entice customers to buy.

"I get bored at the house," he said, following her. "I like what goes on here with the plants, starting new life, watching new plants take over and grow after others have died."

Daphne turned to face him. "Mr. McNary, did you need to buy something?"

He swiped off his hat. "Why are you angry?"

"I'm not angry. I just don't enjoy having a

man follow me around, obviously looking for a woman to fill some unmet need. I can assure you I don't intend to be that person, no matter what you think."

"Daphne, is that why you think I'm here?"

"Aren't you?" The rosebush began to shake violently.

Jack's gaze focused on the large bush and how it wavered. He reached out, trying to grab the pot. The pot fell, breaking the rose in two. Sharp thorns pierced Daphne's hand.

"Oh no!" She began to cry.

"Daphne, I'm so sorry. Let me help." Without reservation, he took her in his arms. He grabbed a handkerchief out of his pocket and began dabbing at the bleeding wounds on her hand. "I have a first aid kit in the truck." He went off to fetch it. In no time, he had his arm cradled around her again. His other hand gently swabbed at the wounds with an antiseptic wipe.

Daphne remained in his presence, sobbing at the broken rose before her and the bleeding wounds on her hand. The tears were more out of frustration than anything else. How this scene illustrated her life right now — bleeding and broken, with thorns piercing her soul.

Rodney rushed out when he heard the

commotion, only to stop short and stare. Daphne glanced up to see his look of surprise and suddenly realized she was in Jack's embrace with her head resting against his shoulder. She wrenched away. "Please leave me alone," she told Jack. "I mean it." She marched into the store and slammed the door shut.

Daphne remained inside the store the rest of the morning, hidden in the back room, unable to venture out after the escapade with Jack and the rose. She hadn't realized it, but when she came in, muttering to herself about the encounter, several customers had been perusing products in the aisles. When they heard the commotion, they came out and stared. Some hurried away without buying anything. Daphne had never been so embarrassed in her life. How she could have made such a scene, and right where the customers could witness her tirade, was too much to bear. At once she placed the blame on Jack. He had put his arms around her, setting her off. That's all he wanted to do in the first place, take advantage of an opportunity to make a move on her. And now she had lost precious customers and money because of it.

Daphne tried hard to look at a memo

book, but the tears clouding her eyes made the words waver like rippling water. How could she ever face the public again? Maybe she should retire right now and let Rodney take over. It would be easier. But Daphne was never one to quit, no matter what humiliation came her way.

Her throat became scratchy from her anguish. She peeked out, hoping to make a cup of herbal tea in the small microwave. A cup of tea was just the thing to bathe her parched throat and calm her frayed nerves. She sneaked out of the back room and toward the microwave, only to find Rodney there, removing a container of food he had heated for lunch.

"Are you all right?" he asked. "I wanted to go back and check on you, but you had locked the door."

"My hand hurts," she admitted. "Thorns can be very painful."

"That was sure nice of Jack to help you like that. He seemed very concerned."

Daphne said nothing but fumbled for a mug and a tea bag.

"He was pretty upset when he left. In fact, he gave me a note to give you." Rodney produced a small note, written on a scrap of paper from a seed company. At first Daphne didn't want it. Glancing up to see

Rodney's questioning gaze, she took it and retreated to the storeroom.

Dear Miss Elliot,

I'm sorry about what happened today. I never want to hurt you. I hope you will forgive me. I didn't mean any harm when I came to see you about a job, but I see that I still manage to upset you, no matter what I do. I want you to know that I won't bother you anymore.

Sincerely,
Jack McNary

Daphne read the note twice. She should feel relieved after what she read, but instead, it made her sad. She remembered how gentle he was after the spill she had taken and how he tried to doctor the wounds on her hand. No doubt he had suffered wounds, as well, with that strange scarring on his face. A man with that kind of disfigurement must have gone through plenty in his life. What he didn't possess in facial characteristics, he most certainly did in his heart. He had been only a gentleman to her. He deserved much more than what she was giving.

Don't go that route, Daphne scolded herself. *Don't think about another man.* She was used to living alone and too old to experience love. It had passed her by as had the years that trickled away one by one, leaving her alone without children or a future. How could she even think of allowing such things to enter her life now?

She turned to find Rodney had come up behind her. From the look on his face, it was almost as if he could read her internal struggle.

"So is everything all right?" he asked.

"He apologized," she said carelessly, hoping her attitude would dissuade him from her real thoughts. "I think he had ulterior motives the moment he set foot on my property."

"Tell me, Miss Elliot — is it so wrong to consider that maybe God might have a special surprise in store for you?"

"If it's a man, I don't want it. You know what happened with that Larson character." Yet inwardly she knew it wasn't true. The scene on the stairs of her nursery told her she did need someone, desperately.

"Larson was a fraud, I admit. But Jack isn't. I've never met anyone more sincere. God must think you need a good man in your life. He's obviously tired of you running the show. Maybe it's about time you thought of someone else for a change."

Daphne gaped at him in astonishment. Rodney had never talked to her this way before.

"And most likely you now regret your decision to pass the nursery on to me," he continued. "But the truth is the truth. And the truth is, you've had so much anger in you that you've never even begun to live. You're like a plant stuck in the same pot of soil. You haven't grown an inch. And if you don't let God try to uproot and plant you somewhere else, you'll shrivel away to nothing." He marched out without his customary song.

Daphne never felt so ashamed. Not only had she caused a scene in front of her customers, but in front of Rodney, as well. Especially after sitting in their home, quoting Bible verses and appearing holier-than-thou, how could she turn around and do this?

Daphne dragged herself home that evening, her mind a whirlwind of mixed emotions. She took Chubs out for his customary evening walk, then returned to the empty home. No longer did the house seem comfortable to her. It was drafty and very lonely.

Daphne went to her room to see a picture of Henry sitting on her bureau. She had displayed the picture of him ever since the day he died in the fire at the lumber mill. He smiled cheerfully at her as he had these past forty years. Daphne exhaled a slow breath. All she had in life was the companionship of some black-and-white photo taken ages ago. A photo couldn't give love or companionship. It couldn't share heartaches and triumphs. And it would never bring her comfort. A photo was simply a memory that faded away with the passage of time.

Daphne kissed her fingers and touched Henry's face in the portrait. She was still bound to the past, as Rodney had said. She needed to start living again and with people who were alive, not dead. She put the picture in a drawer and walked out to the living room. The first thing she would do was call Jack and apologize for her rude behavior. After that, she might invite a few of her lady friends from church for dinner one evening. And she would have Rodney and Melanie over more often. She would open up her home and her heart to others. Maybe these steps would begin freeing her from her root-bound status, as Rodney had put it.

She began by hunting for the scrap of paper with Jack's phone number written on it. When she dialed, an answering machine came on. Daphne hated speaking into machines and usually hung up before leaving a message. This time she forced herself to speak.

"Hello, Mr. McNary. This is Daphne Elliot. I just wanted to say —"

The line clicked, and a male voice came over the receiver. "Hello? Hello, Daphne? Are you all right?"

Daphne straightened in her seat. For a moment she thought she heard a voice of long ago beckoning to her. Goose bumps erupted on her skin. *Ridiculous. Calm down.* "What? I'm fine. Just a few scratches."

"I'm so glad you called. I wanted to let you know that I mailed you some money today to cover the cost of the rose."

"What? But you didn't drop it. I did."

"I had no business asking you about a job. I only wanted to see if you still needed me." He paused. "I just wanted to make sure you had enough help and you weren't overdoing it, especially with that heart of yours. Not that I'm young myself, but I do have a strong heart. At least the doctor told me that ten years ago."

"You should see the doctor every year. You could be suffering high blood pressure and not even know it. That's what my doctor told me. He said many people don't bother to go to the doctor until it's too late and they've suffered a stroke. I can't begin to tell you how many I know have dropped dead from doing the simplest things in life. Though I'm sure you've been to the doctor a few times in your life."

She heard him cough over the phone. "What makes you say that?"

"Oh, well, uh —" She hesitated. Surely he must have been to a doctor with that strange patch of scar tissue on his face, though she didn't want to bring it up and cause him embarrassment. "I mean, everyone has gone at one time or another."

"I've been to doctors, yes, but it's been awhile. Maybe I should go again. Thanks for your suggestion."

Daphne began feeling warm and picked up a small magazine to use as a fan. "Anyway, I didn't want you to think I was ordering you off my property. As it is, I chased other customers away during my outburst. Then I went and blamed you when you had nothing to do with it. You were only trying to help."

He said nothing. All she heard was the soft buzz of the open phone line.

"I guess I'm much too independent and stubborn," she mused.

"And it's my fault."

"Pardon me?"

"That is, I should have realized a woman like you knows what she's doing, especially with running a business. I had no right to interfere. It's amazing to see what you've done."

"Thank you. It did take a lot of hard work." She began to wave the magazine more urgently before her flushed face. "I need to go. Thank you again for your assistance today."

"Anytime you need me, I'll be there. I promise. Just call me."

His words chased her the rest of the evening. She desperately needed help in her loneliness. She needed comfort and security. She wanted peace. Perhaps she really was seeking the love of a good man.

CHAPTER 8

Rodney seemed pleased when Daphne told him about the phone call she had made to Jack. She then promptly invited him and Melanie to join her for lunch the next weekend. He agreed, telling her how much they'd enjoyed the last evening they'd spent together. He then broke into song with "What Now, My Love?" while going about his daily duties.

Daphne continued with an inventory of her existing supplies and readying another order of late-summer stock, including early fall mums and young trees. This time of year, both Rodney and she worked long hours to keep the nursery functioning. The customers liked to come later with the extended daylight to peruse the many varieties of plants and make their selections. Daphne tried to keep her sanity in the midst of the chaos. She dealt with this every year. With the majority of her money coming in during the spring and summer, she threw her entire being into her work. If the truth were known, she didn't have time to be neighborly, like having people over for dinner. The long hours tired her. But since the escapade with Jack and the lecture by Rodney, her conscience bothered her enough to continue with the plans, despite the hectic work schedule.

"I'm really looking forward to lunch," Rodney said a few days later while Daphne's hands were deep in soil, repotting the last of the summer annuals that would go on sale. "Any idea what we're having?"

Daphne hadn't even thought about it. "I don't know. What would you like?"

"Anything you cook will be first-class, I'm sure. By the way, I hope you don't mind, but I'd like to provide the entertainment for the afternoon."

Daphne peered up at him and that ridiculous smile he always wore. He made her feel as if he knew everything that was going on while she stayed in the dark. "I'm sure you're going to sing."

"If you want me to. What would you like to hear? 'Love in Any Language?' 'Lost Without Your Love?' 'Love Me Tender?' "

Daphne took up a small ball of dirt and threw it at him. He ducked, grinning from ear to ear. The soil sailed into the wall with a splat.

"Really, Miss Elliot. That's getting personal."

"What you're doing is getting personal, young man," she added with a smile of her own. "All I've been hearing the last few weeks out of you is love this, love that. And for your information, I think it's beginning to rub off just a tad. I'm trying to show more interest in others. I realize I've been too preoccupied with my own affairs and that something needed to change."

"Hurray! You have so much to offer, Miss Elliot. I remember a saying on a plaque that Melanie once got from a friend. It says, 'Count Your Age by Friends, Not Years.' It's the friends you make in life that count, not how old you are. Which leads me to my after-lunch entertainment."

For a moment, Daphne felt a wave of anxiety creep up within her. If he was planning another scheme like inviting Jack to the luncheon, she feared she might end up in the hospital.

"I'm bringing my laptop."

Daphne paused in her work with her fingers immersed in dirt. She reached for some paper towels. "Whatever for?"

"I need your help."

"My help? I know nothing about those machines. Whatever happened to good old-fashioned handwriting and ciphering? Everyone wants things easy nowadays. They have machines that do all the work for them."

"I need your opinion on something I've been working on. I've been trying to find the identity of a friend, and I've come across practically nothing on the person. It's as if this person never existed."

"Really."

"So I want to share with you what I've found and see what you think. You like mysteries, don't you? I know you read those mystery novels. Maybe you can help me solve this one."

Daphne nearly chuckled, recalling the stack of mystery novels lining the shelf in her bedroom. Yes, she loved a good mystery. Trying to solve a whodunit brightened up an otherwise dull life. But reading mysteries had its drawbacks, too, like drumming up a longing to discover more things about Henry's death in the lumber mill fire. After it happened, the businessmen at the mill remained tight-lipped about the incident for fear of lawsuits. She would never forget the face of one man without a hair on his scalp, looking at her over a pair of glasses. He announced quite matter-of-factly that Henry was in the wrong place at the wrong time. When she asked to see the spot where he died, the man refused, claiming it was under investigation. Daphne followed up with calls to the investigators but was supplied with little information. Everyone said it was an unfortunate accident and that she needed to go on with life. Daphne shook her head. Look where life had led her — a lonely spinster without happiness, entangled in a web of memories.

Perhaps helping Rodney with his little project would be good for her. She could act the role of sleuth, even if this did little to solve her own past. He wanted to play a game, and she would follow along. Maybe he even meant to play the game of Clue, which she enjoyed very much. "Everyone has a past, even if it might be shady at times. Bring your laptop, and we'll see what we can find out."

Rodney nearly leaped in the air before controlling his exuberance to help some customers who had ventured in. Daphne couldn't help but smile. Yes, Rodney was like a son to her, and yes, she was very glad she had signed the business over to his care. If only he would stop with his little match-making ventures and let her live in peace.

Rodney and Melanie arrived a half hour early for the luncheon, catching Daphne off guard. She hurried to finish setting the table with dishes in the pattern of ripe apples. Melanie immediately pitched in to help while Rodney set up shop in a corner of the living room and in Daphne's comfortable chair.

"Miss Elliot, I need a phone jack!" he called out.

"This is ridiculous," Daphne muttered to herself. "Why do you need a phone jack?"

"I have to plug in the modem on my laptop so I can access the Internet. I still have old-fashioned dial-up on this thing."

"I have no idea what you're talking about, but the phone jack is under the table. You'll have to unplug my phone. I don't like being without my phone, though."

"Are you expecting a call from someone?"

Daphne folded her arms. "No, but what if there's an emergency? I'll need to be able to dial 911."

Rodney took out a cell phone from his pocket. "Here. If you need to call 911, you can do it from my cell."

Daphne knew he was mocking her concern but took the phone anyway. She returned to the kitchen, a bit miffed over the encounter, even as Melanie stood by waiting to help.

"It will be another twenty minutes until the casserole is ready," Daphne said.

"May I see your gardens then? When we drove up here, I kept telling Rod how much I wanted to see them."

"You might as well. This will be your home one day."

Melanie looked at her, startled. "What do you mean by that?"

"I mean that when Rodney takes over the business, the house comes with it. You might as well see what I have growing in the garden so you'll know how to care for it. Unless you want to redo it all, which I'd understand. You don't have to keep the varieties I planted."

"But, Miss Elliot," Melanie countered, following her outside, "where will you live if you move out of here?"

"I'm sure a nursing home will take me in." She smiled slightly. "Just kidding."

"That's ridiculous. You will stay here as long as you need to. Rod and I can always look for another place."

"You need to be close to the nursery." Daphne strolled beside the gardens she had spent years planting and tending with a careful hand. Many of the perennials, such as bleeding hearts and painted daisies, were already in full bloom. Daphne explained the different varieties and which plants preferred sunlight or shade. Melanie then admired her selection of roses. Daphne had about a dozen of them, and they kept her occupied during the summer months when she wasn't at the nursery. Already the bushes had tiny buds ready for a showy display.

"These are going to be lovely," Melanie observed. "I suppose you have all different colors?"

"Red, pink, yellow, and blue."

"A blue rose! Oh, I'll have to get myself a blue rose someday. That sounds beautiful."

"The blue is very attractive. You must come over when they are in bloom."

Just then Rodney opened the window to the house and shouted through the screen. "It's ready, Miss Elliot!"

"I guess the timer went off for the casserole." Daphne scurried by Melanie and then Chubs who was asleep on the porch. She was walking past Rodney when something on the computer screen caught her eye. "What are you doing? Snooping as usual?"

"Miss Elliot, you have to come and see," he said as she went on into the kitchen and took out the casserole. "It's about Jack Mc-Nary."

Daphne nearly dropped the heavy casserole dish. She should have known Rodney would be up to something. If there was only some way to tell him to leave things alone. She would have to come up with some good scriptures about allowing the Lord to work and not make something happen out of nothing. But she also realized that love and concern were at play here. Rodney had obviously gone to great lengths to try to be helpful, even if she did consider him a bit nosy. The least she could do was play along while the casserole cooled a bit. And she was curious.

"All right, what is it?"

He pointed to a chair. "Sit down and take a look. I decided to do a little checking on Jack McNary. After that Larson character tried to dupe you once, I thought it would be helpful to know where he's from and everything. And guess what? I found out some interesting things."

Daphne sat with her arms folded.

"For one thing, the man has no past."

"You mean you can't find any record of his past?"

"No, I mean the man has no past. Before I came here, I called around to various record offices. There is no record of the man. In fact, the house he lives in isn't even his."

At this, Daphne straightened in her seat. "What do you mean?"

"It belongs to someone named Stuart Martin."

"They're probably cousins. Or friends. Or maybe he's renting the place."

"Maybe. It would be good to know if Jack and Stuart knew each other. If they do, I think you may have the answers to some of your questions about Henry."

Daphne felt her heart flutter. Warmth crept into her cheeks. "I — I don't understand."

"Rod, can't this wait?" Melanie asked. "You're upsetting her. I told you this should wait."

"No, no," Daphne said, rising to her feet. "What do you mean that Jack might know something about Henry? How could he possibly know?"

Rodney turned back to his computer, his finger sliding across a small black box at the bottom of the keyboard. Daphne watched incredulously as screen after screen lit up. At last he came to Stuart Martin and his personal data. Most of the rectangular boxes she saw remained empty but for a few facts. Stuart had been married to a Melissa Haverston of Tennessee. Rodney then highlighted the man's past work. Employment at the Harrison Lumber Mill near Cleveland, Tennessee. "I did some research on this Stuart. He does have a past, what little I could find. He was once married, and he worked at this lumber mill."

Daphne couldn't believe what she saw. There it was on the screen — the name of the lumber mill where Henry had worked and the same place where he'd died forty years ago.

"I even took the liberty of checking to make sure this was the same Stuart who worked at the mill. I called the Haverston family. They weren't too eager to give out any information, but it seems Stuart once stayed at the boardinghouse run by Mrs. Evelyn Haverston. While he was there, he married the daughter, Melissa. The house where Jack lives was passed on to Stuart by the Haverston family when his mother-in-law died."

"Then why does Jack live in Stuart's house?"

"I don't know. My guess is that they were good friends. Perhaps they worked together at the mill when they were young. Jack may be renting the place from him. If that's so, Miss Elliot, then you need to talk to him and find out what he knows about Stuart and the lumber mill. Maybe he heard something about the accident back in the sixties. I realize it was a long time ago, but this could be an open door to all those questions you've had."

All this came crashing down on her in one terrific storm. Daphne fell onto the couch, too overcome to know what to say or think. Who would have thought the man who frequented her nursery and tended the wounds on her hand with such caring fashion might have a connection to the past?

"Are you all right, Miss Elliot?" Melanie sat beside her on the sofa. "Should I get you something to drink?"

"I — I don't know." She glanced over at Rodney. "Maybe you can talk to Jack for me and find out who this Stuart is."

"I already did. He didn't say much, only that the house is his, fair and square. He seemed a bit miffed that I was prying into his personal affairs. He didn't say it, but I could tell he didn't want me doing any more searching."

"I don't blame him," Melanie said. "This is too much, Rod. You get so involved with everyone else's lives that it really does amount to prying. You need to leave things alone before someone gets hurt. In fact, you may have already overstepped the boundaries."

Rodney gazed at the screen on his laptop. He stared into space for a moment before switching off the computer. "Melanie's right," he said, closing the laptop with resolve and restoring Daphne's phone. "I had no business snooping around. I should've never brought this up. I was only trying to help, but as usual, it comes right back in my face."

The three of them remained still and quiet in the living room, with only the ticking of a clock to serenade the moment. Daphne had not moved since she heard the news that Jack might know something about Henry and the lumber mill. While the past always haunted her, now it seemed to be pointing a finger directly at her. It dared her to make a move and discover the answers to the questions that had bothered her for so long.

Finally she remembered the casserole and went to the kitchen to serve it up. But the joy of the meeting had evaporated, replaced by uncertainty and confusion. During lunch, no one spoke. A rift seemed to have appeared between them all, but Daphne took little notice of it. All she could think about was the lumber mill and the possibility that Jack might have worked there. What she wouldn't give for just a glimpse of the past, if she had the strength to face it.

When Rodney and Melanie were ready to leave that afternoon, he again apologized. "Some entertainment," he said glumly. "I only wanted to do this for you, Miss Elliot, because you've done so much for me." He stuffed his hands into his pockets. "You helped us both and then are giving us the business and all. Believe me, I wasn't trying to hurt anyone."

Daphne patted his arm. "I know. It was sweet of you. You gave me a few things to think about, and it's good to get this brain of mine thinking before it turns to oatmeal."

"Are you sure? I thought I had blown everything."

"No. I must say you did drop a bomb. But I can tell you care. Both of you." She managed a smile, which was cautiously returned. "I'll see you tomorrow." She closed the door carefully behind them, turned to the living room, and suddenly broke down in tears.

Oh, God, after all these years You still remember the pain, don't You? Nothing is hidden from You, is it? You understand and You remember, even when my own memory fades.

I try to keep it all alive with the stories I have of Henry, but I know they are disintegrating with time. Perhaps You truly want me to let go of the past, and Jack McNary is the one who can help me do it.

CHAPTER 9

Daphne didn't sleep a wink that night after learning the news concerning Jack McNary. It was all she could do to keep herself from picking up the phone and asking him outright about Stuart and the lumber mill. For several days, she tried to concentrate on her work at the nursery but kept looking for the familiar truck to roll into the parking lot, bearing the grizzly farmer dressed in dirty overalls. Surely he must have some gardening questions with this being the height of the planting season. Daphne sighed. Although she had apologized for the scene with the rose, she couldn't help but think her attitude might be keeping him away. If so, she could bury any hope of ever knowing what had happened to Henry. She thought back to the conversation with Jack and the final words he offered on the phone. *Anytime you need me, I'll be there.* Little did he know, but she needed him desperately.

She needed to put the past to rest, cover it over with dirt, and place a tombstone on top. She needed the finality perhaps only he could offer.

At that moment, a loud rumbling sound sent her scurrying to the shop window. There came the old truck, the engine noise louder than usual, bearing Jack in his customary straw hat. Even in the warm weather, he still wore overalls and a long-sleeved plaid shirt. Daphne inhaled a quick breath. She felt like a schoolgirl waiting for her beau to arrive. She could have been a young lady of long ago, waiting for Henry to visit her from Tennessee. The comparison nearly made her faint.

Jack greeted Rodney who stared at him for a curious moment before casting a glance at Daphne. Jack then went inside the greenhouse and began looking at the assortment of vegetable seedlings. His thick fingers, stained with dirt, picked up a small, fragile tomato plant. With hands like that, he could easily break the stem in two. But his burly features did not match the heart that lay within. He had only been gentle and kind.

Inhaling a deep breath, Daphne came over and offered a quick hello. He whirled toward her and dropped the plant. Just as she had imagined, the plant snapped in two.

"Another plant destroyed!" He groaned, picking up the pieces and looking at the stem as if considering the possibility of gluing it back together.

"We must be related."

He flashed a look in her direction. He opened his mouth as if to say something, then shook his head. "I'll pay for it."

"No, it was my fault." Daphne took the plant and promptly tossed it in the trash. By this time, Rodney had come to the doorway of the greenhouse, still staring. Daphne wished she could close the door on him. Instead, she turned away and asked Jack how things were going.

"Pretty good. The climbing rose is doing better. The stump I had left in the ground put out new branches. It's looking as good as new. And those plants I bought a few weeks ago are still in the land of the living. So I thought I would try my hand at raising some fresh tomatoes."

"Be sure you have a bed ready for them. Tomatoes like lime and not too much fertilizer."

"I don't know of any plants that don't like fertilizer."

"If you fertilize them too much, they grow only leaves and no fruit. We want fruit, not bushy tomato plants."

Jack leaned against one of the long tables. "You're full of information."

"It's from years of working in the nursery since I was a little girl." Daphne pushed a tendril of gray hair behind one ear, feeling more and more like a shy schoolgirl. Yet in the back of her mind were the lumber mill, Henry, and this man who might hold the key to it all. If only she could ask him about it, but this was hardly the place. She couldn't invite him to dinner. A man alone in her house would be unthinkable. Maybe she could invite him for coffee at a nearby café? Would that be too presumptuous?

"I would like to know more about raising vegetables," he said, "but you must be pretty busy."

"Yes, it would be better to talk at another time."

"Well . . . ," he began, his grayish eyebrows furrowing as if contemplating it all. "I could come back after closing time."

"We close at eight o'clock now."

"Hmm. That means you must eat all your meals here."

"No, actually Rodney mans the place in the evening. I leave at five o'clock."

"Is that a fact? Well, then, maybe we can grab a bite to eat after work. What about that interesting restaurant in Charlottesville — the Hardware Store Restaurant? They've got those good specials on weekdays."

"All right. That would be fine."

Jack McNary gaped at her as if stunned that she had so readily acquiesced. Warmth invaded her face. Perhaps she shouldn't have appeared so eager, but the knowledge he had was too important to her right now. Surely he would understand it all once the purpose of the meeting came to light.

She hurried away to find him a box in which he could put some tomatoes and other seedlings. Inside the store, Rodney was sorting out insecticides when she came to the cash register.

"So are you two going to meet?" he inquired, gazing out from around the aisle.

"Yes," she answered. "And it will be your fault if things go bad."

"I'll take full responsibility. I already said I was sorry about the intrusion. In fact, you don't need to pursue this if you don't want to."

"Oh, you're a fine one to be telling me this now, after that so-called entertainment at my house! What am I supposed to do? Just forget everything you said?"

Jack suddenly appeared inside the store, carrying the box of plants.

Daphne ceased conversing with Rodney and began adding up the plant purchases, hoping Jack would not notice her trembling fingers. "Twelve dollars and eighty cents."

Jack shook his head. "That can't be right. I bought fourteen plants. Let me count them." He did so and nodded. "Yep, fourteen, and the sign back there said a dollar twenty-nine a pack."

"Well, don't worry about it. It was my mistake." Daphne held out her hand for the money.

He laid two tens in her hand. "Keep the change."

Daphne stared in astonishment. When he winked at her, her fretfulness disappeared, replaced by a strange sensation. Many men had winked in the past, but his gesture was different — as if he appreciated what he saw. Her gaze followed him as he went to his truck and placed the box carefully in the front seat. He then stood and stared back at the nursery, almost as if he were studying her, as she was him. He then climbed into the truck and sped off.

"So what do you think?" Rodney whispered in her ear. "Nice guy, eh? Perfect, as a matter of fact."

"I'm not thinking about that right now. I only want to find out what he knows about the lumber mill. In fact, we're going out to dinner." She clamped a hand over her mouth. "Oh no! We didn't agree on the day! I don't know if it's this evening or not. What am I going to do?"

"Wait a bit till he gets home, then call."

"I–I'm certain he meant tonight." But she wasn't sure about anything anymore. Her hand went to her heart as it began to flutter like a butterfly in her chest. *Oh, Lord, I have to resolve all this. My heart can't take much more. Help me.*

The phone rang at the nursery later that afternoon. Daphne was grateful it was Jack, asking her what time he should pick her up for their dinner that night. She told him five-thirty, as she would need to change and take care of Chubs. He seemed enthusiastic about the meeting, saying he was looking forward to learning more about vegetable gardening. Little did he know, but she was looking forward to learning more about Stuart and the lumber mill.

As she dressed, she thought about how she might broach the subject. It would seem a bit out of the ordinary to mention the past suddenly. She had learned from Rodney how irate Jack could be if she went fishing for information. There must be a way to handle this tactfully. Daphne looked at her image in the mirror. How the years had crept up on her, along with the developing wrinkles around her eyes. She had tried some of those wrinkle-reducing agents but found nothing that worked. For a time, she dyed her hair also, but the chemicals became too irritating and the bill at the beauty parlor too expensive. Her hair was gray with strands of pure white scattered throughout. Was she even attractive to a man anymore?

Daphne picked up a bottle of foundation and applied a light coat. She remembered how her mother always made herself pretty for her father, even if she was working side by side with him in the nursery. She wore a thick, pasty type of makeup and bright red lipstick. And her father seemed to enjoy having Mother look her finest, even when working in the dirt. Daphne didn't relish the idea of looking made up for a man, especially to impress Jack. But if it lent some confidence to the night and helped her discover the past, then she would be the most made-up woman on the planet.

The doorbell rang. Daphne's heart skipped a beat. She checked her appearance once more in the mirror. At the last moment, she took out the pearl necklace and fastened it around her neck. Nodding her head, she scooped up her purse and headed for the door. The first scent she caught was not the scent of roses or honeysuckle, but the aroma of a powerful aftershave. She hadn't smelled aftershave like that in years. Before her stood a different man from the one she'd observed roaming about the nursery. Gone were the overalls and straw hat. Instead, Jack wore a pair of tan slacks, a red polo shirt, and shoes that shone in the final rays of the fading sun.

"I have to lock the door," Daphne said in a trembling voice, turning to fumble with the key.

He offered her his arm to guide her to the car, but she held fast to her purse strap and ambled along on her own. To her surprise, an old Lincoln Continental replaced the dirt brown truck in the driveway.

"Are you really Jack McNary?"

He cast her a quick glance. "Why would you say that?"

"I just want to make sure you don't have a twin brother. I was expecting to have my first ride in a truck."

He chuckled and opened the door for her. "No. I rarely take this car out. Only on special occasions."

For a moment, she wondered if Stuart might have left the car behind for him to drive. She peeked around the vehicle for anything that might have Stuart's name on it, even as Jack gave her a strange look. When he asked her to get his sunglasses from the glove compartment as the last glimmer of sunlight pierced through the windshield, Daphne opened it and began shuffling items around. She hoped for a car registration or something with Stuart's name.

"Can't find them?"

She sheepishly handed him the glasses case. "I like to see what people store in their glove compartments. Why they call it that is beyond me. There's barely enough space to put a pair of gloves inside." She quickly closed the small door and sat back in her seat, staring out the window. She tried to think of the questions she wanted to ask tonight, but already it seemed as if Jack had grown suspicious of her activity. For a long time she stayed silent as they drove to town. Finally she decided to forge ahead. "So have you lived in this area long?"

"About five years."

"Where did you come from before that?"

He drove into the parking garage. "I hope they can find us a nice, quiet place. Do you prefer a booth or a table?"

"A table," she said as they entered the

restaurant. "The seats in a booth are always too far away from the table. At a regular table, you can at least pull your chair up close enough without having food spill on your lap."

Jack asked the waitress for a quiet table. They were led to a table for two in the rear of the restaurant. Daphne began feeling more uncomfortable when she saw the lit candle and even a rose in a crystal vase.

"I wanted to say you look very nice tonight. The pearls are beautiful."

"Oh yes," she said, fingering the strand. "A friend gave them to me."

"Oh, really?" He hid his face behind the menu the waitress had given him.

Daphne smiled at the waitress and asked her for a glass of water. She opened the menu book, but the words seemed to float about on the plastic-coated paper. She prayed she wasn't having some kind of spell. Likely it was the atmosphere and the eyes of a man staring at her from across the table. "Yes. He died a long time ago."

He put the menu on the table. "I lost my wife about five years ago, as I told you. I moved here to start over. But she loved eating out. I think she would have liked a place like this. Homey. Low prices. And not a buffet."

Daphne couldn't help but laugh. "Most of the food places in town are now buffets. I once counted over twenty Chinese restaurants in the phone book one day, of which more than half were a buffet. It's a waste for people like us. One plate and I'm full."

The waitress arrived to take their orders. Jack gave hers first, then his. "So you don't like Chinese?" he continued.

"I don't like the MSG. Bad for the heart. But what I really don't like are the fixed prices for buffets when I can barely eat a plateful. Rodney took me to a buffet once. I told him it was a waste of money. He only smiled. Have you seen the way he smiles? Just like a cat who swallowed the canary. Sometimes he bothers me to no end."

Jack laughed as if he took great delight in her grumbling. How she wished she could sound happier. Even as she spoke, she could hear her words — complaining, critical, bordering on bitterness. Is this the way she had been all her life? No wonder she was a spinster.

Daphne grew silent while the waitress placed the food on the table. Jack bowed his head and offered the blessing for the meal. After he finished, he delved into his salad. "I must say, I don't have a problem with food. I like most places. Steak houses, barbecue pits, even pizza."

"I get heartburn just thinking about it," Daphne added before realizing she was doing it again. "That is, I used to like pizza very much until it kept bothering me. The doctor finally gave me a prescription for it. I take a pill every night." She stole a glance at his face, and the scar that seemed more pronounced with the overhead light shining on it. She wondered how he received such a disfigurement. It wasn't from some kind of machine. It looked more like a patch, as if the skin's surface had been stripped away at one time and then replaced.

"Is something wrong?"

"Oh no, I was — I was just thinking about where you might have lived before you came here. You said you moved here five years ago."

"A neighboring state. Tennessee."

Daphne nearly choked on the lettuce in her salad. She quickly took a sip of water. "Then it makes sense."

"What makes sense?"

"What Rodney told me."

At this, Jack slid back in his seat and crossed his arms. "Now look, Daphne. I'm not sure what's come over that young man of yours. If you ask me, he's got a nose too big for his own good. He called me the other day, asking me all kinds of questions, like he was trying to investigate me or something. Do you know why he's doing this?"

"He's curious, I guess," Daphne said, playing with the lettuce leaves and tomato wedges on her salad plate. Finally she decided to come out with it. "Actually we were both wondering if you knew a Stuart Martin while you were in Tennessee?"

Jack had been sipping water. He jostled the glass, sending water running down the front of his polo shirt. He grabbed a napkin and wiped his shirt. "You're treading in private waters."

"Rodney discovered you don't own the house you live in and that it belongs to someone named Stuart Martin."

He said nothing as he continued to wipe away the water, then asked the waitress for another glass and more napkins.

"So he called Stuart's wife's family."

Jack jerked his head upright. His face turned the shade of ripe strawberries. "What? What did they say?"

"Not much. Only that Stuart used to work at a lumber mill." Daphne could not hold herself back. "I need to know if this Stuart worked at the same mill back in the sixties. It's very important. Someone I knew died

147

in a fire there and —"

"Daphne, we came here to have a nice dinner and talk about vegetables, not about lumber mills, Tennessee, Stuart, Evelyn —"

Something within Daphne snapped to life. She had not mentioned Evelyn's name. Jack did know something. She opened her mouth, ready to inquire, when she saw an angry look form on his face. Things were beginning to deteriorate. If she wasn't careful, she might lose everything she'd hoped to gain. For now she forced down her questions about the past and offered a brief apology. Yet Jack seemed to disappear inside himself. He said little during the main course. Daphne tried to talk about planting vegetables as he wanted, but the conversation felt forced. They finished their dinners, having talked about little else.

Jack drove Daphne home in silence, except for a few brief comments about the lack of rain. When he dropped her off at the door, Daphne felt worse than ever. She could barely unlock her door before collapsing onto the sofa. Chubs was at her side, yipping to be let out. Daphne didn't have the energy. She could only think about the night. She knew she had made a mistake by being so headstrong in her quest for knowledge. Instead of drawing out the answers, the questions had driven back whatever lay within Jack McNary. Now everything was lost.

CHAPTER 10

Daphne arrived for work the next day, worn-out after last night's escapade. She nearly called Rodney to ask him to keep tabs on the place while she spent the day in bed. She decided against it, realizing she would only lie there recounting the conversation between her and Jack. As it was, she didn't sleep a wink from thinking about it. She sat out in the living room, looking at old photographs while Chubs slept peacefully at her feet. One picture depicted Henry at the mill, standing beside several coworkers. She scanned the other men carefully with a large magnifying glass, wondering if any of them might be Stuart or even Jack. Oh, what she wouldn't give to know the truth. At times she wondered why she couldn't let this rest and go on with life. But God must have resurrected the past for some reason.

Daphne dragged herself into the nursery

that morning, sipping on a cup of coffee which she knew was a no-no. But if she didn't drink it, she might fall asleep. Rodney was his usual perky self as he strode into the store, smiling from ear to ear.

"So how did it go?" he asked. "I'll have to admit, I was up practically the whole night wondering what happened. You don't know how much I had to restrain myself not to pick up the phone and call you for all the sugary details."

"We ate dinner, and he brought me home," she said, putting bills and change into the cash register.

Rodney groaned with a sound that startled her. In an instant, her heart began to flutter. She found herself gasping for breath and immediately sat on a stool. "Really, young man, must you do that?"

"I'm sorry, but you're giving me a heart attack. Please tell me what happened."

"You think you're having the heart attack? With the kind of stress I've been under lately, it's a wonder I'm not in the cardiac ward of the hospital." She opened her purse and took out a vial of nitroglycerin.

"Please — what happened?"

Daphne put a pill under her tongue, hoping it would relieve that terrible sensation in her chest as though butterflies were fighting to fly against a harsh wind. "I already told you. We went to the Hardware Store Restaurant. We had dinner. Then he took me home."

"Did you talk about Stuart?"

"I mentioned it, but he wasn't interested in talking about it. So I let it go." Out of the corner of her eye, she could see the expression of dismay on Rodney's face, as if she had allowed a huge opportunity to pass her by. "But he did mention Evelyn," she added hastily. "That is, he mentioned her name, and I hadn't even said anything about her."

"Really! Very interesting. Evelyn ran the boardinghouse where Stuart stayed, you know. Eventually Stuart married Evelyn's daughter."

"Oh, and I found out Jack is from Tennessee."

Daphne thought Rodney was going to leap over the counter with the way he began jumping. "Aha! I knew it. That proves it then."

"Proves what?" Daphne placed her hand on her chest, feeling her heart race beneath her fingertips. At least there was no pain, but the continual fluttering made her nervous.

"My original train of thought — that Jack knows Stuart and Stuart worked at the lumber mill in Tennessee. Now all we need is for Jack to tell us about their friendship and if Stuart worked at the mill during the time of Henry's death."

"He won't do it," Daphne stated. "It bothers him for some reason. In fact, he wasn't very happy when he dropped me off last night. I think he's tired of people poking their noses into his personal affairs. And I must say, I can understand it. If someone were prying into my business, I would be upset, too. I might even notify the authorities."

"Don't you want to know what happened?"

Daphne wondered right now if she did. The idea had seemed intriguing at first. But perhaps it wasn't the best thing to have all the knowledge in the world. After all, God forbade Adam and Eve to eat of the tree of the knowledge of good and evil. Sometimes He didn't want His children knowing everything about a situation. Maybe He felt it wiser to keep it from her. If the truth about Henry's death were known, it might create such an emotional strain that she could have a heart attack. For whatever reason, the knowledge of the past had been kept secret. "It's best to let it go," she said with a weary smile as several customers began trickling in to start off another busy day at the nursery. "There's a reason for it. So let's do what we do best."

Rodney said no more, though at times Daphne caught him looking at her in a strange way as if disappointed by her decision. She felt it the wisest thing to do under the circumstances. Life's challenges were hard enough without her trying to take on more than she could handle. And this was definitely a burden she couldn't begin to carry on her own.

The day went fairly smoothly with a steady flow of customers, but Daphne felt that she might need to close up shop early. Her heart continued to act up. She suffered a strange numbness in her left fingers and occasional twinges of pain. If there weren't a letup in these symptoms, she would call the doctor. Dr. Franklin was very particular about her condition. She liked him very much, especially the way his mustache twitched when he said "Miss Elliot." He was also very thorough with his examinations. No doubt he would see her after hours if her heart did not settle down and behave itself.

Melanie arrived before closing time, dressed up for her date with her husband. Since the argument that had brewed a few weeks before, Rodney made it a point to take Melanie out on special dates, even if it was for a walk. Daphne observed the couple from afar when Rodney came toward Melanie with his arms outstretched. He scooped her up, hugging her close, his lips searching hungrily for hers. Daphne shook her head. Tears invaded her eyes. There was nothing sweeter than young love, like the birds that fluttered around the old owl's head in *Bambi.* Daphne often commented that she couldn't take Rodney's love songs, but deep down inside, a part of her yearned for a similar kind of affection. The only man who had held her since Henry was Jack, after the rose thorns pierced her hand. His was a gentle but strong touch, much like the memory she once had long ago.

Rodney and Melanie drew apart and smiled sheepishly. "I was telling Melanie about the dinner you had with Jack," he said, bringing Melanie's hand to his lips for a kiss.

She giggled and stole her hand away. "I'm glad you both got together, Miss Elliot."

Daphne smiled. "It was nice, I suppose. So where are you off to tonight?"

"Pizza and maybe a movie. You want to come along?"

Daphne laughed. "Three is definitely a

crowd. This is your special night. Have fun."

"We will." Rodney gave a wink before slipping his arm around Melanie and serenading her out the door to the tune of "Love Me Tender."

Daphne had to chuckle before a yawn nearly split her head in two. At least her heart calmed down enough for her to finish her work. She only needed to complete the bookkeeping for the day; then she would go home, take a nice hot bath, and go straight to bed. The figuring was slow to come when Daphne realized how exhausted her mind had become. Finally she gave up on it, promising to finish it when her head was clearer. Night shadows had already begun to fall across the landscape when she fished for her keys.

All at once, she heard the thump of footsteps on the porch of the shop. A familiar voice called her name. Her heart began its frantic fluttering once again.

"Daphne? Daphne, are you in there?"

She drew forward to find Jack standing there with a Thermos in his hand. What on earth was he doing here? After last night, she had not expected to lay eyes on him for a long time. But there he was, dressed like the evening before in a polo shirt and slacks. She hoped he wasn't here for another out-ing. She was too tired to think straight. "Do you need something? I'm closing up shop."

"I know it's getting kind of late." He stepped through the door and looked around at the dark interiors but for a small lightbulb dangling over the cashier counter. "I was hoping we could talk."

"I didn't think you were in the mood to talk," Daphne said in more of a huffy tone than she would have liked.

"I'm sorry for the way I acted at the restaurant. I guess your questions hit a nerve."

Daphne returned to the books, suddenly energized enough to rework the figures. All it took was Jack McNary to spur her to life. Usually it was something on the side of irritation, but now it was curiosity. Her hand patted the flutter in her chest that began again in earnest.

"I know things haven't been right since I first came to your store." He pulled up a stool. "So I took it all to the Lord last night and asked Him what to do."

Daphne listened with interest.

"He said I needed to come clean, to stop with the charades, and to tell it like it is."

Daphne continued to bend over the book, wondering what he was talking about.

"So you really don't want to hear what I

have to say?"

Daphne put down her pencil. "Jack, I did want to learn more about you; yet when I tried to ask, it was as if I had committed a crime."

"So what do you want to know?" He sat back, crossed his arms, and waited.

For once, Daphne was speechless. She had spent the last few days planning out all the questions she wanted to ask him. After the fiasco of last night, she had pretty much dismissed them all, until now when the door had suddenly been thrust open.

"You wanted to know if I knew a Stuart Martin in Tennessee," he began.

Daphne felt herself growing nervous. "Yes."

"All right, then. Stuart is me."

Daphne blinked in astonishment. "What? You mean you're Stuart?"

"Yes, and the house where I live, the one your employee, Rodney, was trying to figure out about, does in fact belong to me. I decided to make some changes in my life when I moved here."

"I guess so, if you were once Stuart and now you're Jack. I don't know what to say."

"The reason I changed my name is because of what happened to me at the Harrison Lumber Mill."

158

At this, Daphne stood up. "You did work at the lumber mill! The same mill!"

"Sit down and let me explain." He brought out two cups and poured some tea from the bottle. "I knew you liked to drink tea, so I made up some fresh."

Daphne smiled shyly before picking up the cup, only to find her hand trembling. There was something in Jack's eyes she wasn't sure about. He stood on the verge of confessing everything he knew; yet she wondered if she had the strength to face it. He was there, at the Harrison Lumber Mill, the same place where Henry died. She wanted to know everything, even if it meant going through the fiery past herself, with smoke that burned her eyes and heat that singed her flesh.

"I did work at the mill on the day of the fire. At first it seemed like an ordinary day, but somehow I knew it wouldn't be. Maybe it was the Lord getting me ready. The fire broke out in the area where we were cutting up the logs. It was suspicious from the start. My face was burned pretty badly. I went for help and came across a boardinghouse owned by Evelyn Haverston, a few miles down the road. She took me in, got me a doctor and everything. It took quite a bit of doctoring to manage the burns. I didn't think I made out too bad, considering."

Daphne stared at the scar prominently displayed on his face before resting her gaze on his eyes. There was something in those eyes that seemed to plead with her. She shook her head. She was so intent on finding out what was going on that she was letting her emotions get the better of her.

"After awhile, I got to know Evelyn's daughter, Melissa, and eventually came to love her. We were married and lived in the area for quite a few years. Occasionally the family would come back here to Virginia, since they owned a summer home. Five years ago, I lost Melissa to cancer. It was very hard. Not long after that, Melissa's mother, Evelyn, died, too."

"I'm sorry," Daphne managed to say. "I know what it's like to lose a loved one."

Jack glanced down at his lap, examining the cup he held in his hands. He tried to speak but found himself choking. He took a sip of tea. "Anyway, Evelyn left me the summer home in Virginia in her will. And that's where I've been living."

"It is hard to lose the people you love. They all say you get over it, but you never do. So did you know Henry Morgan at the mill where you worked? Can you tell me what happened?"

"I — well —," he began, suddenly flustered. "I had my own problems that day, believe me."

Daphne leaned forward. "Did they tell you how the fire started? Did you hear if anyone had died?"

"I left after it all happened and never looked back. I haven't put my foot on the place since. I'm sorry."

She tried hard to contain the tears that welled up within her. The most promising lead into what happened to Henry had suddenly vanished. How she wanted to break down and grieve for him once more, especially after this disappointment. She sniffed and fumbled for a crumpled tissue inside her purse. "I can't blame you for not knowing what happened to Henry, but I had such high hopes you did." She looked up to see the scar on his face turning a bright shade of pink. "It must have been awful to be in a fire like that and suffer such a terrible burn."

"The disfigurement was the worst part. In one minute, I had lost all of my characteristics. I thought I would never be good enough for another living soul. What woman would want to be with a man like that?"

"Oh, it's not that bad. If we all dwelled on the tiny flaws in each other, we would never see the good on the inside." She shook her head. "And that's all I've done my whole life, finding flaws and not looking at a person's heart. Maybe it's better that I am an old spinster. I don't think Henry knew what he was getting."

"I'm quite sure he knew."

Daphne choked out a chuckle. She took out her wallet and from it a crumpled photo of Henry at the mill. "Here he is, doing the work he loved best. I will never forget the last day we had together. I wish now I had said certain things to him. You can think of a million things to share after a loved one has passed away. But what good is it?"

Jack put down his cup. "Daphne —"

"It's all right. I shouldn't be burdening you with this anyway. That's all I've been doing, burdening you and everyone else with my problems. I want Henry here — sometimes I even believe he's here, but of course he's not. I'm sure you understand, having lost your wife."

"Daphne —," he began again.

"It's like this ache that never goes away. Maybe that's why I have a heart condition. It's an ache I can't seem to get rid of. I was hoping you had the answer. I was praying that —" She stopped. Her throat tightened. She put her hand over her mouth to silence it. "Excuse me. This isn't right. It's wrong to place this all on you."

"Daphne, it's all right. It's more right than you can think. I —" He paused. Slowly he took out his own wallet.

She dried her eyes on the tissue. "Oh yes, do you have a picture of Melissa? We can share in the memories, can't we, if nothing else in life."

He took out a crumpled card from the wallet and handed it to her.

Daphne took it and blinked once, then twice. "I don't understand. This is Henry's driver's license. How did you get it?"

"Daphne . . . my name isn't Stuart or Jack. It's none of those. I–I'm Henry Morgan."

Daphne dropped the card.

"Daphne, please, let me explain what happened —"

"No, no, no." A terrible pain gripped her. She came to her feet, wavering. "You left me — you're dead. I know you're dead! You've been dead forty years! How can this be happening?" A sudden weakness overcame her, the weakness of a burden she had carried for too long. Her knees began to buckle.

Jack tried to reach her, even as she fell to the floor. "Daphne!" he cried, kneeling beside her, cradling her. "Daphne!" He shook her gently.

"No, no, no." She moaned until Jack's face disappeared in a cloud of white.

CHAPTER 11

Dear God, help me! The words repeated over and over in singsong fashion, but in another time and place. Daphne moaned and shifted about, struggling with both the reality of Henry's existence and the terrible game that had been played on her emotions. She could see Henry as if it were only yesterday — young, handsome Henry, his bearded face all smiles as he took her hand in his. How strong and warm his hand felt, though calloused by the heavy labor at the mill. Yet she wasn't afraid to have that hand hold hers and his lips press ever so gently on her own.

Daphne moaned again. Suddenly she remembered the news of the dreadful fire, the men who were injured and, yes, the death of her beloved Henry. She flicked open her eyes to see a pure white ceiling above her. Maybe she had died, too, and was now in the presence of the Lord. She

165

struggled to sit up, only to find herself hampered by plastic tubing coming out of her arm. Strange metallic wires ran beneath her simple gown and were hooked to a monitor by her bedside. Heaven could not be like this. It seemed more like a horror movie instead.

A woman wearing a flowered-print smock and blue starched pants stepped beside her, holding a strange contraption. A probe was forced into her ear. Daphne nearly screamed at the obtrusive thing but let the machine do its work. The woman then attached some kind of monitoring device on her forefinger.

"I'm just taking your blood pressure and temperature, Miss Elliot," the woman re-assured her.

No, she was definitely not in heaven, un-less the Lord had a ward of nurses at His beck and call. The Bible said she would have a new body one day and not this worn-out model that had endured so much heartache and pain. Suddenly she shook at the scene that came to mind — of Jack taking out that old crumpled card, yellow with age, to display the name still inscribed on it: HENRY T. MORGAN.

"You need to relax," the nurse told her. "Your blood pressure is rising."

Daphne wanted to say that hers would

skyrocket, too, if she had just been informed that her sweetheart from forty years ago had suddenly been resurrected from the dead. But she felt too tired and dazed to say anything. Even a whisper would take every ounce of energy within her, though her mind was a bundle of questions. Maybe she had dreamed up the whole scene with Jack. Maybe inwardly she had hoped he would be Henry. She didn't want to admit it, but she had feelings for the man. He was irritating yet comforting. He was craggy yet kind. Then she thought about it. The eyes. The voice. They had been teasing her the weeks she knew him, but of course it never dawned on her that he was actually Henry. Henry had a beard, black hair, a trim figure. Henry was dead. Now he had come back to life.

"Oh, God, help me," she managed to sputter. Her fingers groped for the leads on her chest that monitored the beating of her frazzled heart. How much more of this could she take? The Lord would help, but at this moment, she felt herself teetering on the brink of despair or maybe even death. If something didn't happen soon, she would be lost. She knew it.

At that moment, a parade of doctors assembled in her room. The scene caused her to shake once again.

"Miss Elliot, I'm Dr. French," said the lead doctor. "Your case was referred to me by your physician, Dr. Franklin. I have a few medical students with me today on rounds. I hope you don't mind them observing while I discuss your diagnosis and treatment."

Daphne did not have the energy to speak. She simply nodded her head. What did it matter anyway if these young people studied her like a mouse in a cage? She was in a cage after all, a cage of emotion with no way out. Her hand went to her heart as it began to flutter. The students pointed at the monitor and murmured to themselves. At least she was giving them a good show.

"Miss Elliot, your heart is undergoing severe strain at the moment," explained Dr. French. "You've been throwing what we call PVCs. That means your heart is not beating correctly. We have an electrical system within the heart that helps each chamber beat at the correct time. Sometimes when part of the system fails, the heartbeat becomes irregular and the heart can't perform its job. What we want to do is take you for a heart catheterization to see if anything might be causing the irregular heartbeat. If we find that the electrical system within the heart is malfunctioning, we can put in what's called a pacemaker."

"I've heard of that," Daphne croaked.

"Good. Then you know it's a simple procedure with excellent results. The nurse will provide you with instructions concerning the catheterization procedure. Of course, as with any procedure, there are risks involved." He took out his clipboard. "The condition could worsen; there might be extraneous infection, bleeding, heart and/or vessel damage, or death, though of course that's unlikely. Do you wish us to proceed?"

Daphne could only nod. Slowly she placed her signature on the document, allowing the procedure. The doctor nodded and paraded away with his flock of students, discussing the necessity of the procedure and what was involved. Daphne turned to the window to see a few clouds drifting by in the blue sky. She blinked back the tears that filled her eyes. Why was all this happening to her? Obviously God had a plan. Maybe He was trying to soften her hard heart by making it malfunction. Or maybe He had a better plan for her, and for now she must endure this. If only she didn't feel so alone.

A tear slipped down her cheek. If she died on the table during the procedure, who would care, really? Rodney and Melanie might be sad for a time, but then they would inherit the business. Perhaps Rodney would come and lay a wilted rose on her grave. But soon she would be a forgotten memory. All her hopes and dreams, everything about her, would be buried away forever. There were no children to carry on. It would be as if she'd never existed.

A nurse came in with an instruction sheet for the heart catheterization, along with a scrub brush soaked in an antiseptic solution to ready her for the procedure. The nurse looked at her for a moment and asked if she was in pain.

Daphne wanted to tell her that life hurt and maybe death would be better than living.

"Many people have gone through this procedure, Miss Elliot," the nurse explained. "It will help the doctors determine what the trouble is."

If only you knew, Daphne thought. *I have so much trouble in my life. I have a business in the height of the selling season that I can't manage. And Henry is both alive and dead. Oh, my dear woman, you don't know the trouble I have.*

"When I feel as if things aren't working out, I like to take time and pray things through," the nurse said.

At these words, Daphne felt a sudden burst of energy strengthen her.

"It makes me feel better if I can release it all," she continued.

"Yes," Daphne managed to croak out. "I– I'm a Christian."

The nurse smiled. "I thought so. I don't know how, but I had a feeling you might be. You remind me of my mother. She had heart trouble. But she always smiled and trusted in God. Eventually when it was time for her heart to be at peace, she went to heaven praising God. I know she is praising Him still. It helps me to think about her and realize that in tough times God gives the strength we need to get us through."

Again the tears began to fill Daphne's eyes. *Dear God, You sent an angel to my bedside.* Nurses were often called angels of mercy, but Daphne truly believed God had sent this young woman to encourage her. Even if she were all alone and no one else was there, God was. God knew everything that was happening. He knew her fears, her questions, her confusion, and her pain. He was ready and willing to bear it all in His strong arms.

When the nurse finished prepping her for the procedure, Daphne felt peace descend on her. She decided to let go of Jack and his wild tales and concentrate on getting well. It was the only thing she had the strength to do.

The nurse squeezed her hand. "I'll pray for you," she whispered.

"Th–thank you," Daphne managed to say, even as the orderly came to wheel her away. She was still frightened, but she felt peace. She was weak, but her spirit was strong. Even when she was wheeled into a large room with personnel hurrying about, arranging instruments, she felt the prayer of the nurse God had sent.

Daphne arrived back from the procedure, dizzy and sore but grateful to be alive. On her hip, she felt the pressure of a sandbag a nurse had applied to prevent bleeding from the site where the catheter was inserted. Nurses came by often to check her blood pressure and the machines clicking by her bedside. She looked around for the nurse who had prayed with her but discovered she had gone off duty while Daphne was in the catheterization lab. Now all she could do was wait and find out the test results.

A young nursing assistant walked in, carrying two flower arrangements. Daphne sucked in her breath when she saw them. Part of her hoped one of the arrangements might be from Jack, while the other part wished it wasn't. The first was from her church family, the other from Rodney and Melanie. The aide also gave her a note. Daphne took the letter and slowly opened it.

Dear Miss Elliot,
I know you wanted to give me the business, but I'm not ready yet. So you have to get well soon!

Daphne couldn't help but chuckle at Rodney's opening statement, even if the motion caused pain in her hip. She continued reading.

Don't worry about a thing. Melanie is my acting assistant, and she's doing a great job. I only had to scold her once when she didn't arrange the seed packets the way you like them. But really, she is doing a great job. There's something about having the love of your life working by your side that makes things run smoothly.

Daphne began to heave when she read the words "love of your life." Her hand fell on the bed, though her fingers still held tightly to the letter. Who was her love now? Jack?

Henry from the past? Both Jack and Henry? Neither? When she felt her heart begin to act up, Daphne drew in a deep breath to calm herself. She refused to entertain such thoughts.

I was sorry to hear what happened to you but glad Jack was there to help. He called me at home and told me what happened. I would have come to the hospital last night, but they said you were too ill for visitors. I will come this evening if you feel better and sing you some songs. And, I promise, no major bombshells. I only hope I didn't cause all this.

Daphne shook her head. "Of course you didn't," she murmured.

So just relax and get better. Everything is going great here. But I miss you.

Love,
Rodney and Melanie, my assistant

Daphne slowly folded the letter. No doubt Rodney would do well on his promise to entertain her when he arrived. It wouldn't surprise her if he came with a full-fledged orchestra, ready to accompany his singing.

How like a son he had been in so many ways. She was glad, very glad she'd made the decision to give him the business. And it might come sooner than any of them expected, especially if her heart couldn't take the strain.

Just then the parade of student doctors dressed in white lab coats returned, headed by young Dr. French. Daphne tried to remain relaxed when she saw the contingent, but it was difficult. There was no telling what the diagnosis might be. For all she knew, he might be coming to tell her it was hopeless, that she would never recover, that the wounds of the past had caught up with her and she would soon die from it all. If only she had found Chubs another home before she passed on. Who would care for him?

"Just as I suspected, Miss Elliot," the doctor said nonchalantly. "We found it necessary to put in a pacemaker to regulate your heart. The bandage on your chest will be there a few days. We put in dissolvable stitches."

Daphne didn't realize there was a bandage on her chest until her hand felt something soft and bulky beneath the hospital gown.

"We will monitor you for a few days, then send you home. You did very well."

"So I'm not going to die?"

"You have many good years left, Miss Elliot, if you take care of yourself. I can tell you are a strong woman. And I know for a fact you run an excellent business."

A surge of excitement raced through her. "You do?"

"Of course. My wife has bought all our summer roses from your nursery. And I must say, they are beautiful. Now of course you will need to take it easy for a few weeks. I hope that assistant of yours can mind things for a time until you've recovered. After that, I must insist you cut back on your work schedule, if not consider retiring altogether."

"So you really think I can't go on."

"You'll go on, Miss Elliot. You just can't keep doing everything as you used to. At one time or another, we have to let the younger ones take over. And I think your heart has been saying that the past few years. Okay?"

She couldn't help but smile at him, especially after the wonderful news that he and his wife were loyal customers at the nursery. Watching the group depart, she rested against the pillows, mulling over what he had said. Things would be different now. Just how different, she wasn't sure. At least she thanked her intuitiveness in settling her business affairs before all this came up. The stress of having to find a successor to the business might have forced her back into this place. She wondered if Rodney was ready to accept the reins of owning a business so soon. He would surely appreciate the extra income, as would Melanie.

Daphne continued to think about the plans she must make in light of this new information, when a nursing assistant came into the room bearing another vase of flowers. This time they were roses with a bluish tint, to Daphne's amazement. How often she recalled telling others she preferred blue roses to red, despite their oddity. At that moment, she thought of Henry. He knew how much she loved the single blue rose he once brought her long ago.

A strange sensation came over her. When the aide gave her the card that accompanied the bouquet, she immediately tensed. The wound on her heart began to ache. The tape on the bandage pulled with the straining of muscle. She heard the beeping of the heart monitor take off like a galloping horse. *I can't read this. I'm not ready.* She nearly called the nurses to have them take the bouquet away, until curiosity got the better of her. For all she knew, Rodney might have surprised her again with a pretty arrangement. Maybe she had told him she loved blue roses. She couldn't remember, with all the talk of plants they'd had over the year.

Her fingers shook as she tore open the envelope.

I'm so sorry, Daphne.

Jack

It was not signed Henry but Jack. She looked at the dozen blue roses surrounded by baby's breath. She put the note on the nearby nightstand, even as tears began to collect in her eyes. He knew exactly what to send her — because he knew her from long ago.

CHAPTER 12

"Time to get up and get going!" came a cheerful voice.

Daphne had just begun to drift off to sleep when a deep voice awakened her. She was glad for the wake-up call, as her dream had begun to center around Henry and the first time he brought her a bluish-colored rose. Initially she had been upset the rose was not red. All young women in love were given red roses, or so she thought. But there was something intriguing about that rose. It was different. The color reminded her of the soft mist that occasionally shrouded the mountains. He had searched high and low until he found someone who had grown them experimentally, as such roses did not exist in those days. It was a rare find and extremely costly. It showed love beyond measure.

She blinked open her eyes to see past the blue roses arranged in the cut-glass vase to

Rodney's smiling face. Behind him stood Melanie.

"Oh, Miss Elliot, are you all right?" Melanie asked, drawing up a chair to her bedside. The feel of the young woman's hand on hers was like a soothing balm. It nearly made her cry.

"I–I'm a machine now," she whispered.

Melanie glanced at Rodney. "I don't understand."

"They put a pacemaker in my chest to control my heartbeat."

Rodney waved his hand as he drew up a chair next to Melanie. "Oh, that's nothing, Miss Elliot. They do that kind of procedure all the time. Even governmental officials have pacemakers. 'It takes a licking and keeps on ticking.' "

"Now I won't take any more of your jokes, young man," Daphne managed to say but with a small smile. Before her sat her children, even if they weren't flesh and blood. No mother could be prouder. "So how is the nursery?"

"Doing well. We're making good sales. People have come by asking about you."

"Which reminds me," Melanie added. She opened her purse and withdrew a stack of envelopes. "People have also been dropping off cards. Some asked about sending you flowers, but since you run a nursery, they decided it might not be the best thing. So I'm collecting the cash and will get you a gift certificate at the mall or something."

"What? I don't understand."

"Guess you don't realize how much you're loved until the going gets tough, eh?" Rodney winked before turning to the roses. "And what a smashing bouquet! Who's the secret admirer? Let me guess."

Daphne turned away. "Please don't say it." Out of the corner of her eye, she saw Rodney sit back in his seat as if he had been slapped. "I'm sorry. I wish I could tell you things, but I can't."

"You don't have to say a word, Miss Elliot," Melanie said, patting her hand while shooting a glare toward Rodney. "You've been through so much. You need to rest and take it easy. How long will you be in here?"

"A few more days. They want to make sure the pacemaker is functioning properly."

"Hospitals still smell the same," Rodney piped up, recovering after Daphne's remark. "I'll never forget the time my parents brought me in kicking and screaming after I fell off my bike. I needed thirty stitches in my head. I broke my arm, too."

"You never told me you broke your arm," Melanie said.

"Sure did. Right at the elbow." He rolled up his shirtsleeve to display the jagged scar.

"I thought you had only cut yourself."

"Surprise."

Daphne tried to concentrate on their conversation, but all she could think about was the scar on Jack's face. The fire had caused it, or so he said. But if he really was Henry and he had been burned — why didn't he tell her? Why did he run away, leading her and everyone else to believe he was dead? Why did he change his name? And then he married another woman to boot! All of it began a slow, steady simmer of anger that increased as time went by. Nothing of what he'd told her gave the real reason for his actions.

"Can you do me a favor?" she asked Melanie.

"Of course. Anything."

"I would really prefer it if you took those roses home with you. They are — well, I'm getting a headache and think I may be allergic to them."

"Allergic to roses?" Rodney declared. "You work around them all the time, Miss Elliot."

Daphne gritted her teeth at the young man who could see through her like someone peering in a shiny plate-glass window.

"It must be something new." Rodney shook his head as Melanie agreed to take them, exclaiming how beautiful they were. When Rodney asked who sent them, Daphne refused to say. He let it go and began discussing the business, including how to handle the new shipment of plants scheduled to arrive in the morning. Daphne tried to relate the business details as much as she could but soon grew weary from the visit.

"She needs her rest," Melanie told Rodney. "Before we go, we did bring you a present. Maybe it will make the time go faster."

Daphne took the gift, unwrapping it to reveal a mystery novel. "Thank you."

Melanie leaned over and planted a small kiss on her cheek. "You take care of yourself. And don't worry about the nursery. We have everything under control."

"I'll try not to. Just keep your eye on Rodney."

"Hey!" Rodney said indignantly. "I know exactly what I'm doing. After all, if I'm to be the heir to the throne one day, I'd better know what I'm doing. Take care, Miss Elliot. We'll try to stop by tomorrow."

"Don't forget to take the vase of roses."

Melanie picked them up, again exclaiming

over their loveliness, before telling Daphne good-bye.

She watched the bouquet disappear behind the closed door, hoping and praying that everything else would likewise disappear. She looked at the mystery novel in her hands. Life itself had become a mystery. Maybe someone someday should write a book about her. She certainly had a tale to tell. Daphne pressed her eyes shut, wondering how everything would be resolved in the end.

Daphne slept little that night after the visit by Rodney and Melanie, too overcome by anxious thoughts to relax. The next day, she was encouraged to get out of bed and walk around a bit. The doctor monitored her heart rhythm and blood work carefully, announcing that she was recovering nicely. She could go home in a day or two if everything continued to check out. This news brought about a new set of worries. How would she care for herself and Chubs once she arrived home? For now, Rodney had been letting Chubs out and feeding him. Perhaps she would have her strength back in a few days. But a simple shuffle to the door of her room and back had all but worn her out. If her energy level didn't return soon, she might have to hire someone to help. The mere thought went against her independent nature. God was certainly doing a work in her, both in the natural and the supernatural. All the ideals, beliefs, and traits she had worked up within herself were being beaten down. She wanted to throw up her white flag of surrender, if not for the thin wall of pride keeping humility at bay.

Daphne heard the nursing assistant come in, bearing a tray of food. She was a sweet girl, not more than twenty years old. She had told Daphne how she was in this job to help pay her way through college. Daphne admired her spirit. It was good to see a young person labor to achieve her dream. Daphne had worked hard also, but had her dreams been achieved? Glancing out the window, she couldn't help but disagree. Her hopes had been dashed so many times she couldn't keep count. The only reason she took over the nursery in the first place was because she couldn't bear the thought of her brother selling it. If any dreams were left to be had, even in her older years, she prayed God would soon bring them to fruition before it was too late.

Daphne slowly pushed the button, bringing the bed to an upright position to stare at the food. All the rumors of hospital food had come true as she tried to eat the unrecognizable mass of beef stew. Finally she gave up and had only the gelatin and decaffeinated coffee.

The door to her room opened. A visitor. At first she couldn't see who it was, until an image slowly came into focus. A man stood there holding a huge arrangement of flowers.

"Hello, Daphne," the voice said slowly, setting the arrangement carefully on a table.

No! Not him! She couldn't take it. Her mind grew foggy. Her head began to spin. "P–please leave."

"Daphne."

"I mean it. I'm trying to be nice, but I feel terrible."

"I do, too. I'll never forgive myself for what happened."

"I — I don't like what happened either, but right now I feel terrible. I didn't sleep very well, and the food here is awful." She fumbled for the call button, only to find a pillow had slipped between the mattress and the controls on the side rail. She tried to jerk it out.

"Here — let me get that for you."

She allowed Jack McNary this one act of kindness. He took out the pillow, laid it on the bed, then stepped back. He stood there, staring intently for several moments with his hands planted in the pockets of his trousers. Again he had dressed nicely for the occasion. She stared, trying to imagine the scar replaced by a beard he'd worn in his youth. If she didn't feel so horrible at that moment, she would ask him to smile and see if he really was Henry. But the thought made her sick. She knew perfectly well who it was and that he had abandoned her for another. He had left her alone, by herself, lost in memories for forty years.

Jack looked around the room. "The nurse at the desk said some roses had come for you."

"I gave them away."

He inhaled a sharp breath. "Why?"

His simple question caught her off guard. "Because — because — I didn't want them."

"Daphne, did you see what color they were?"

She wanted to tell him they were pink or white or any other color but blue. She knew what he was hinting at. He meant for her to accept what he told her that afternoon in the nursery, that he was her long-lost love. "Please — I need some rest."

"Daphne, if only you could hear the rest of the story."

"I know what happened. You pretend to be dead, make up stories, then end up marrying someone else. You — you leave me alone, miserable, a spinster until I'm old and gray and my heart is broken. And you think time heals. Well, it doesn't." Just then she felt a stabbing pain in her heart. Her finger pushed the call button.

Immediately two nurses appeared in the room to assess her pain while a dumbfounded Jack stood nearby. Daphne could see the tears welling up in his eyes. She didn't care. She had cried more tears than he could ever hope to cry, even if he did it every day for the rest of his life.

"You need to relax, Miss Elliot," the nurses told her.

"Please ask him to leave," she said, pointing to Jack. "He's upsetting me."

One of the nurses acknowledged him. "Sir, I think it would be a good idea."

Jack looked as if he were about to faint. He turned as white as the sheets on the hospital bed. He staggered backward. "Daphne —," he groaned, then turned and walked out the door.

"Please don't let him visit me anymore," she told the two nurses.

Yet the voice that uttered her name echoed in her mind the rest of the evening.

CHAPTER 13

Daphne slept poorly the next few nights in the hospital, distressed over the encounter with Jack and the way everything was turning out. He tried once more to visit her when the head nurse of the unit stopped him and made him surrender the teddy bear he had brought. Daphne asked the nurse to keep it at the station to accompany the bouquet that decorated the counter. She wanted no more reminders of the past. Maybe after this he would understand she needed time and to leave her alone. He had to realize he couldn't make up for forty years while he was married to someone else. Daphne ground her teeth at the thought. She knew she must try to avoid stress, but Jack McNary had succeeded in foiling any plans for peace and tranquility. On top of it all, she had other stresses to deal with — the nursery business, keeping her home, and caring for Chubs.

Daphne gingerly drew on a button-down blouse over the small bandages covering the wounds from the surgery. She still felt weak and run-down, but the doctor had decided to discharge her. He gave her strict orders not to return to work for several weeks. Maybe she could ask Rodney to continue walking Chubs before and after work, but he had already done so much. For a fleeting moment, she considered Jack. He would do anything she asked, but it was better for both of them if he stayed away. Even as she put on her slacks, she thought of all those photo albums of Henry in her home. Now she would have to get rid of everything. There would be no more memories to tease her now that the truth had been exposed. Still, she was left with the unending question, *Why?*

The young nurse who had shared the scriptures with her before she went for her heart catheterization now came to give her discharge instructions. As Daphne listened patiently to all the dos and don'ts, she wished the nurse also had instructions on how to deal with life.

"I'm sure you're glad to be leaving us," she said with a smile.

"Yes and no," Daphne admitted. The nurse's eyebrows arched in surprise. "What

I mean is, I have a lot to think about once I get home."

"Just remember that you need to take it easy and avoid stress. That's why I gave you the brochure on stress."

"My dear, if you only knew what my life is like right now, you would see that's impossible."

"Miss Elliot, what is impossible with man is possible with God. And He is very good at carrying our burdens."

Daphne almost kissed the nurse on the cheek but nodded and smiled instead. She waited patiently until the orderly came to wheel her downstairs. Melanie would be picking her up and bringing her home. She was rolled along in the wheelchair and saw the huge bouquet and a teddy bear decked out in a red bow sitting on a counter at the nurses' station. It cheered the place up immensely, she had to admit. No doubt Jack was trying to do the same in her life. She stared at the bear for a moment. He was sweet, with his head tipped to one side as if asking what troubled her. But no flower arrangement or cuddly bear could diminish the storms that tossed her to and fro. If Jack thought flowers were a recipe for sunshine, he was wrong.

Melanie was waiting for her as promised,

with a smile on her face that eased Daphne's misgivings. God had been good to give her these two young people who were like a son and daughter. She hoped she wasn't being a burden.

"How is the business?" she asked as Melanie helped her into the car.

"Don't worry about it, Miss Elliot," Melanie said. "Rodney is a very good businessman. I think it's in his blood."

"He does show quite a bit of promise, I must admit, even if he does wander about in a love-struck fog at times."

Melanie couldn't help but chuckle. The drive home took about thirty minutes. Daphne marveled at the changes to the scenery during the week she had been in the hospital. Summer had descended on the hills and dales. The trees were full and leafy. Early summer blooms brightened up the yards. Wildflowers planted in the median of the four-lane highway cheered her. When Daphne arrived home, she found her gardens vibrant with a showy display of flowers. She sighed in contentment. Everything looked better than she had anticipated. The barking of Chubs from inside the house was like music to her ears. Using Melanie's arm for support, she got out of the car and began walking slowly to the house.

"I'm as weak as a newborn kitten," she professed in dismay. "What am I going to do?"

"Don't worry about a thing," Melanie told her.

Upon entering the house, Daphne was astonished to find a bed already made up for her on the sleeper sofa. A stack of mystery novels, checked out of the library, rested on a stand. From inside the kitchen, she detected the aroma of soup on the stove. And decorating the fireplace mantel was an assortment of flowers in vases.

"I — I don't understand —," she began.

"Welcome home," Melanie said, squeezing her hand. "I decided to make up your bed here in the living room where you can read or watch television. That way you won't have to climb those stairs to your room."

"Isn't that sweet."

"I also bought a better mattress for your sofa bed. It should be more comfortable for you."

"What?" Daphne asked in bewilderment, eyeing the bed before her. "I'll pay you back. Let me know how much it is."

"It's a gift," she said.

"Melanie, you know you can't afford it."

"No, I mean it. Your church got together and took up a collection for it. So it really is

193

a gift. They also brought over all kinds of food. Your freezer is full."

"Isn't that sweet," Daphne said again. Tears formed in her eyes. It never dawned on her that members of the church would care that much. It blessed her to see the outpouring of generosity at a time like this.

"Just make yourself at home. I'll go check on the soup."

Melanie went off to the kitchen, humming to herself. Daphne watched from the living room as the young woman slipped on one of Daphne's frilled aprons and took up a spoon to stir the soup. God had indeed been merciful and kind, even when she didn't deserve it.

Slowly she went and lay down on the sofa bed. My, how good a firm mattress felt to her weary body. The pillows were covered with the cases of embroidered blue roses she had buried away in her linen closet. She rested there, thanking the Lord for bringing her home alive, even if her spirit was troubled by all that had happened.

Her gaze fell on the familiar features of the living room before coming to rest on the fireplace mantel. She had pictures of her family displayed there, including one of Henry. Vases of flowers now stood among the pictures. At the end rested a faded photo of Henry, standing stiff and proud, with barely a smile teasing his youthful face. Next to it was a small vase with a single blue rose.

The sight of it angered her. With all the energy she could muster, she went over and took the vase off the mantel. "Melanie!" she cried.

Melanie hurried out of the kitchen. "What's the matter? Are you all right?"

Daphne nearly shook the vase in front of her face. "What is this doing here?"

"I thought you would like it. The roses were so beautiful that I thought it would be nice to have one on the mantel."

"Yes, but why is it sitting next to the picture of Henry?" She began to shake. Melanie rescued the vase before she dropped it and gently helped her back to the sofa. "I'm so sorry," Daphne mumbled. "I don't know what's the matter with me."

"I think you've just been through a major illness, Miss Elliot, and your body is telling you to rest."

"I — I think so. And please call me Daphne. I can't stand the thought of being a Miss. I wish —" She paused. The emotion caught in her throat, choking off her words. How could she tell Melanie that deep down inside she wanted to be a Mrs.? She wanted

195

a man to care for her and love her. She wanted to fix him meals and raise a garden together. She didn't want to be alone the rest of her days. Inwardly she wanted Jack, but she was too stubborn to admit it.

"You'd better lie down," Melanie said, coaxing her to the sofa. Daphne did as she was told. To her dismay, Melanie returned the rose to the mantel beside the fading portrait of Henry. Then she left the room to dish up some soup.

Daphne glanced over at the cabinet where she kept her photo albums. Slowly she reached for an album that held her treasured memories. Settling back on the sofa, she opened up the first page to a close-up of Henry. She studied it for some time. Jack, she knew, was plumper and his hair gray, along with that unsightly scar on his face. He had no beard as Henry used to wear. But now she could clearly see a familiarity in the shape of the eyes and the broad shoulders. The comparison sent goose bumps riding along her arms. She flipped through a few more pictures, mostly taken from a distance with Henry doing his favorite things. One picture showed him with a croquet mallet over one shoulder. Daphne paused, thinking about the croquet game she and Jack had played at the church picnic. Jack had been a gentleman through and through. And if what he said was true, Henry himself had sat across from her at the table, commenting on her fruited gelatin salad. The very idea made her shudder. She shut the book with resolve, scolding herself for doing this when she knew better.

Melanie returned, carrying a tray with a bowl of soup and some crackers. She glanced at Daphne with a strange look on her face. No doubt Daphne could imagine what she looked like. "Are you all right?"

"Yes, just doing something I wasn't supposed to."

"Now, Miss Elliot, I mean, Daphne, that's why I'm here. I arranged things so I could spend a few days with you. I'll take care of everything. I don't want you overexerting yourself and ending up back in the hospital."

"I'll try to be good," Daphne said with a smile, looking at the chicken and rice soup that Melanie had prepared. "This doesn't look like canned soup."

"Oh no. I followed my mom's recipe."

"How wonderful." Daphne took a taste. "This is delicious, but I don't want you slaving over me and going to all this trouble. You have a life to live rather than taking care of a fussy woman."

"Daphne, you've been like a mom to both

of us," she said, settling into a chair. "I know Rod appreciates everything you've done. And since his own mom died a few years back, you've meant a great deal to him."

Daphne chuckled. "I thought I was only a bee in his bonnet."

"It's okay. He could use a jolt once in a while. But, honestly, you've been so helpful to us. I know how much you cared about our marriage, especially when you came to visit us that one night. It meant a lot to us. I realized then that God did bring Rod and me together for a special reason. I had no right to tear us apart just because things weren't working out the way I'd planned."

Daphne rested the spoon inside the bowl. The words jabbed at her like the tines of a fork. Isn't that exactly what she was doing with Jack? Perhaps God had brought them together for a special purpose; yet she was batting it away. Daphne shook her head and tried to eat another spoonful. Melanie watched her as if trying to analyze her thoughts. At least the young couple didn't know anything of what went on between her and Jack. Rodney would have a field day with it if he knew.

At that moment, a knock sounded on the door. "That's probably Rodney," Melanie said with a smile, rising to her feet. Chubs began to bark, drowning out the greeting that was taking place in the foyer. Daphne continued to eat until she felt a presence enter the room. The strength was so tangible that she could nearly touch it. She glanced up, and there he was. She dropped the spoon inside the bowl. Though her flesh wanted her to look away, her spirit remained mesmerized, especially after the pictures she had just seen in the photo album.

"I wanted to make sure you got home safely," he said slowly.

"Yes, thank you." Her face reddened when his gaze traveled to the mantel. No doubt he saw the blue rose resting beside the picture of Henry. *Did he think I did that? I hope not.* "If you don't mind, I'm feeling very tired."

"Please stay and have a bowl of soup," Melanie offered to Jack, running to fetch him some.

Daphne watched in a daze as he took a seat opposite her, in the chair where she often sat and gazed at photo albums, reminiscing about days gone by. If only she had the strength to run away from this embarrassing scene. She would take Chubs for a walk, go upstairs to her room and lock the door, anything rather than see this.

Melanie returned with the soup. Jack

gulped it down in several swallows, to Daphne's amazement. He acted as if he hadn't eaten in a week.

"I really do need to get some rest," Daphne said in as controlled a voice as possible.

"I understand. I just wanted to say I was sorry for what happened in the hospital."

Oh no, not in front of Melanie! I don't want her to know he's Henry. Daphne's heart began to race. "I'm feeling very tired," she said once more. "I — I think I'm getting heart pains again. I don't want another spell."

Jack rose to his feet. "Daphne, if I could only tell you about —"

"Please, not here, not now. I have to safeguard my health. Please go." She turned away and closed her eyes.

Jack said no more. He bade a quick good-bye to Melanie and left.

Melanie stared wide-eyed, first at the closed door and then at Daphne. This was just the scenario Daphne wanted to avoid. Jack had brought up all kinds of questions in Melanie's mind, which she would take to Rodney. And Rodney would not give her a moment's peace until he knew everything.

Without a word, Melanie took her tray and retired to the kitchen. She said nothing about the encounter. But Daphne thought about it the rest of the evening, wondering why God was doing this to her and at a time when she felt so weak.

To Daphne's relief, Melanie never mentioned Jack's visit. Instead, she was busy caring for Chubs, cooking up the meals offered by the church members, and taking care of business. Rodney came by in the evenings to advise Daphne about the nursery and to cheer her up with his usual playful antics. One evening he sang while Melanie accompanied him on the guitar. Daphne had never heard a more beautiful duet. After the performance she told them they should make a CD with a Christian recording company, to which they both shared loving glances. When Daphne saw them kiss good night in the foyer of her home, she thought of Jack. There had been no word from him since the day he'd left the house. Daphne figured the end had finally come for them. He had been chased away from more places than a mouse. But her life's book still had blank pages left to be written on. She had no idea what the future held. Even though the blue rose had long since faded away, she had the distinct impression that something else lay ahead of her. Only God held the answer.

Melanie called Daphne for dinner inside the kitchen. After a few days on the sofa, Daphne insisted on eating her meals at the table. She didn't want to be an invalid for the rest of her days. Melanie had warmed up the last of the beef stew brought over by a member of her church. Daphne sat down at the table, bowed her head, and began to eat. "Aren't you having any?"

"I hope you don't mind, but Rod is picking me up. We're going out to dinner."

"How nice. Where to?"

"Believe it or not, to the Hardware Store Restaurant." She nearly laughed out loud. "It seems strange, but we really like that place."

Daphne stopped eating. The Hardware Store Restaurant was one of Jack's favorite places. She wished her a pleasant evening. "And after tonight, you can go home," Daphne told her. "I can take care of myself now."

"Are you sure?" Melanie asked. "At least I'll come over for an hour or two and make sure Chubs is all right."

"That would be wonderful, thank you." Daphne stared out the back window, lost in thought. She hated the idea of being alone in the house. She enjoyed having Melanie around. It made her feel young again to sit and chat about womanly things over cups of tea. She was grateful Melanie never mentioned the scene with Jack. Instead she talked about her flower business and how she hoped one day to make it thrive. It was during that particular conversation with Melanie that Daphne suggested she sell some flower arrangements at the nursery. Melanie hugged her afterward.

"It's the least I can do after everything you've done for me."

"Daphne, you know I don't want you paying me back. We're supposed to be there for each other."

But Daphne couldn't help paying her back in some small way. Without Melanie and Rodney, who knew what might have happened to her?

Just then a car sounded in the driveway. Rodney came to the door, all smiles as if eager to spend the evening with his love. The aroma of aftershave filled the house. Daphne watched the two of them kiss. How she would love enjoying a relationship like that, if only it were meant to be.

"So did you tell her?" Rodney asked in a low voice, loud enough for Daphne to hear. She had a keen sense of hearing and could distinguish even the slightest sound.

"Tell me what?"

Both Rodney and Melanie turned to face her. "We've been talking —," Melanie began.

"Actually we've been talking to Jack," Rodney corrected.

Daphne felt her face grow warm and her heart begin to thump. No doubt the pacemaker would have to kick in with what was about to come out of Rodney's mouth.

"I think you need to talk to him."

"I will take it under consideration," Daphne said icily.

"There's more here than meets the eye. If you only knew —"

"I know plenty, and what I found out landed me in the hospital."

"You can't blame Jack for your sickness," Rodney exclaimed.

Daphne bristled. He was right, of course. And she owed Jack an opportunity to explain, as he'd tried to do many times.

"We care about you, Daphne," Melanie said. "And so does Jack."

"And we also know he's the one you thought was dead long ago," Rodney continued. "It's amazing. A miracle, really. I think you owe him a chance to explain why he did what he did."

"I don't owe him anything. In fact, he owes me forty years. Forty years of grieving for a man who wasn't even dead! Forty years of thinking he had been burned alive when he was married to another woman."

Rodney sighed. "You know I can't tell you what to do. But you were very good when you came to us during a hard time in our relationship. Maybe now you can use a bit of your own wisdom — how we need to trust God even when things don't look right. Melanie and I, we were only looking at things through our eyes. All I want you to do is think about Jack through God's eyes. And use a bit of that faith you were telling us about. See if maybe there are things you hadn't considered — like healing those scars you both have right now."

Daphne stared, dumbfounded, as the couple headed out the door. She returned to the sitting room, exhausted by the verbal battle with Rodney. Yet his words rang true. She had not looked at any of this through God's eyes. She had imagined all kinds of scenarios with regard to Jack and not once considered there might be other possibilities. He wanted to tell her the facts, but she refused to listen. She thought about the scar on Jack's face and how it changed colors with his moods. She wondered about the pain he must have gone through, suffering such a wound. And maybe like her, he had scars within that also needed attention.

She pondered it all until her eyelids grew heavy and sleep won her over. Soon she was dreaming of Henry during their final meeting before the fire. She appealed to him to consider moving to Virginia, even working at the nursery.

"It isn't time yet, Daphne."

"Of course it is! Who knows what the future holds? And we love each other."

"Daphne, when that time comes, I'll know. I'll come back for good. And when I do, I will gather you in my arms, and we will get married. I promise."

Daphne flicked open her eyes in a start. The lamp on the table shone full in her face. Had the time come? Had Henry returned at last, ready to fulfill his promise?

CHAPTER 14

Rodney was surprised to see Daphne at work the next morning, shaky but determined to help him with the summer rush. When he asked about her health, she brushed the question aside and put on her best smile for the customers who came to select flowers and other plants. She knew what he was thinking, that she had ignored both his advice and her health to satisfy an obstinate heart. He said little, only inquired about a new shipment of late-summer plants that included the fall selection of brightly colored mums.

"Also, I hate to mention this, Miss Elliot, but I cut myself a check while you were in the hospital. It was close to payday, and since I knew you couldn't do it, I went ahead and paid myself. You know how Melanie gets if I don't pay the bills on time." He showed her the ledger and the amount he had deducted.

"You don't have to justify your actions. In fact, I plan to give you more for the management you did while I was sick."

"You don't have to do that."

"A worker is worthy of wages," Daphne said with a smile. She pulled out the check ledger and began writing him a check when the door to the shop burst open.

"Rodney, can you give me a hand?" the voice called out. The man stopped short and stared. When their gazes met, Daphne felt a rush of warmth flow through her. He quickly turned and left. Rodney threw her a look before leaving his post and walking after him. Daphne came to the window, just in time to hear Jack mention how he didn't know she had returned to work.

"Don't let that stop you. You need to interact."

"And I told you I won't come unless she asks me. I made myself a promise. I won't chase her anymore. I was wrong to do it in the first place."

"It isn't wrong to show her you love her. And, believe me, she needs all the TLC she can get, even if she won't admit it."

Daphne hung her head low at these words. She desperately craved love, even if she was stubborn and hardhearted. She once thought love meant her place of business, her dog, or her life as an independent spinster. But now other things were at work, other emotions she never would have dreamed could bubble up after so many years.

She peeked out the window to see the sunlight shining full on Jack's face and the scar he said he suffered from the fire. Is that why he left, because of the scar? Is that why he found comfort and purpose with another woman, believing she wouldn't want him anymore? If so, he was foolish to think it. A man was not a machine that could be thrown away over some insignificant defect. She would have received him with open arms, even if he had two heads and twelve fingers. She had been madly in love . . . once. If only he hadn't run away as he did.

"I do appreciate everything you young people have done," Jack said. "I believe the Lord used you in this situation, even if it isn't turning out the way I'd hoped."

"Hang in there, Jack. Things will change. Just be patient. I've learned by working in this place that patience is definitely a virtue."

He chuckled. "I've been learning it also. I've waited a good long while for the Lord to work on my own heart. I think about how patient He's been with me. I can hardly say a word against Daphne and her response in the situation. As she's said, it's been forty years. But I know coming forward as I did was the right thing to do. You see, Rodney, when God resurrects something in one's heart, it's meant to happen. And I know the love is there. I believe we're meant to be together, somehow, some way."

His words melted Daphne's heart. She walked to the rear of the shop and took a seat, pouring tea she had made into a cup. Tea. The truth had come out in the conversation she and Jack shared over cups of tea. What would become of it all now?

Daphne returned to writing out the check to Rodney when he came back inside. She sensed his thoughtful perusal, but he made no mention of the encounter with Jack. Instead, he showed her a list of bills that needed to be paid and the profit secured within the last month. Daphne was pleased to see how her business had been blessed, even with the topsy-turvy spins and twists in her life. It also confirmed to her that Rodney was indeed an excellent choice to take over the nursery when she retired. Both he and Melanie had done a wonderful job. She owed them a great deal. If only she could be sure what her own future held.

He paced back and forth, wondering what to do. His hand sifted through his gray hair. Yes, Henry was very much alive. He had kept the man hidden away for forty years, but the truth was begging to be released. She had to know the truth. And she had to know he'd done it to protect her. If only she would let him tell her what happened, to let the confessions come forth, to make her realize that even if he had loved and married Melissa, it didn't mean he cared for her less now than he had so long ago. He didn't want to be an old widowed farmer the rest of his days. He wanted to be her love and her husband.

How I long for you, even after all these years. I know I was only a memory, a picture you would gaze at in the darkest of nights. But I've come back. I'm alive. I've been alive for forty years, even if I spent much of my life with a woman whose companionship I cherished. After Melissa died and the years began falling away one by one, I knew God was resurrecting you in my heart. I remember our walks in the rain, the ball where we danced, the tender touch of your soft lips. Yes, the years have passed. We are no longer the same people. It may even be too late. But I truly believe love can be renewed, Daphne, with God's grace and mercy.

He flicked away a tear, as he laid aside his thoughts and rose to his feet. He would try one more time to reach Daphne's heart, even if it was concealed behind a stone wall. He would try once more to see if love might be there or if it had disappeared with the passage of time.

The meeting she overheard between Jack and Rodney affected Daphne more than she realized. The words shared had been tender and sincere. Even now she reflected on it and the meaning behind it.

But I know coming forward as I did was the right thing to do. You see, Rodney, when God resurrects something in one's heart, it's meant to happen. And I know love is there. I believe we are meant to be together, somehow, some way.

Did he truly mean what he said? Did he think their love would last a lifetime? Or was he hoping not to be alone for the rest of his life after losing the woman he married? All these things spun around in Daphne's mind in an endless circle. She could hardly eat that night or even read one of the mystery books stacked by the sofa bed. She could do nothing but sit and think about Henry the young man, Jack the mature man, and herself caught in between.

When the doorbell rang, she almost didn't hear it. Only Chubs's incessant barking made her rise to her feet and shuffle to the door. She peeked out between the blinds to see him standing there, as big as life itself. Her breathing nearly ceased. What was he doing here? She hesitated, watching him. He stood still, waiting patiently. He obviously knew she was there. She also knew if she didn't answer that door he would be gone forever.

Almost in a daze, Daphne opened the door.

Startled, Jack took a giant step backward and nearly fell off the porch. "Hello, Daphne. I — I probably should have called and told you I was coming." He faltered. "I know you don't want to see me, but if I don't get these things out in the open, you will never know the truth."

"I — I don't like strange men in my home," she said, "especially in the evening."

"I was going to ask Rodney to come along. If you want, I'll call him and ask him to come be a chaperone of sorts."

"No, never mind." What she didn't need right now were two men giving their opinions on how she should think and feel. She opened the door wider and allowed him inside. Glancing around the living room, she noticed she still had the portrait of Henry sitting on the mantel. She tried to ignore it and took a seat on the sofa. Jack appeared melancholic as he sat down stiffly in her favorite chair. His eyes were dull. There was no cheer in his facial features and certainly not in the scar where the light of the lamp illuminated the ragged edges. He looked down at his fingers intertwined on his lap.

"There are some things I must tell you, Daphne. But before I do, I hope you will believe me when I say that I am Henry Morgan."

Daphne looked away to focus her gaze at the framed portrait of a smiling Henry. A lump formed in her throat. "It's hard for me to believe that. For all I know, you could be a clever imposter out to dupe me. It's happened before."

He shook at the statement. "Daphne, please don't say that." Pain laced his words. "I will tell you then how much I loved the waltz more than any of those other fancy moves. I gave pearls to a beautiful woman one Christmas and walked along a bridge overlooking a quiet river. I blew kisses so she might catch every one." He inhaled a deep breath. "And I told her that when I returned to Virginia I would marry her."

Daphne's knees began to shake. This couldn't be happening. Too much had changed. They were not the same people. Even if the memories were his as well as hers, she didn't know if she loved him. She was in love with a young and vibrant man, one who cared for her and would do anything for her, except the night of the fire. "Why did you fake your death at the lumber mill?"

"I didn't fake it. The authorities believed I was dead. There was no trace of me found, except for a few personal belongings. I ran off and found refuge at Evelyn's boarding-house. I was hurt. My face was a mess."

Daphne crossed her arms. She had heard all this before.

"Daphne, they wanted me dead anyway. It was better for everyone to believe I was dead."

At this, Daphne looked at him in confusion.

He leaned forward in his chair, intently focused on her without wavering. "You see, I was about to tell on the corporate bosses. They were involved in extortion and embezzlement. I found out the scoop through some careful detective work I'd done at the mill. Fellows at the mill were upset there had been no pay raises in several years, even though the company profits were skyrocketing. Someone somewhere was pocketing the extra cash and not giving it to the workers. I found out who it was. I was about to become the greatest whistle-blower the company had ever seen."

Daphne managed to draw a breath and remained riveted on his story.

"The bosses heard about it. They threatened me, trying to keep me silent. But, worst of all, they threatened you. They were going to use you to keep my mouth shut. I didn't know what to do. I wanted to warn you, to tell you to stay away, that there were men who wouldn't shirk at hiring assassins if they could to keep their money and their lifestyles. So I waited. I prayed. I asked God what to do. So many times I wanted to call you and tell you what was happening. I felt so alone."

Daphne had to admit she would have been scared if he'd told her strange men were threatening her life. Silently she thanked the Lord he hadn't told her. Just the idea sent her shivering once more on the sofa.

"Are you all right? I'll stop if you want me to."

"No, I'm fine." She took the afghan off the back of the sofa and wrapped it around her legs. "Go on."

He hesitated.

"I want you to go on," she added.

He relaxed a bit. "Anyway, I considered letting you know what was happening when the explosion occurred. It wasn't an accident. Something sparked inside the chain saw when I turned it on. The thing blew up in my face. I was thrown nearly forty feet, and I hit my head against a tree. I think I was knocked out for a while. When I woke up, a fire had spread into the woods. My face was so raw and painful that I didn't know what to do. When I realized what had happened, I took off into the woods. If they were trying to kill me, I didn't want them to think I was alive."

"So you pretended to be dead?"

"I didn't tell anyone one way or the other. I just ceased to exist. It was the safest thing to do. I walked for miles that night and reached Evelyn's boardinghouse at daybreak. I wasn't even sure how far I went. When I got there, I told the family my name was Stuart and that I had burned myself working on some machinery. I never told them about the fire at the mill. From that moment on, Henry Morgan was no more.

Evelyn was able to find medical care for my face. They heard there was a fire at the mill. They had some questions. But I refused to tell them I was involved and stuck to my story. I didn't want them in on what had happened. Evelyn's daughter, Melissa, helped me a great deal. A lot of nursing was involved, and Melissa did it all. She was a trained nurse. In time we did get married, and for the next thirty-five years, I was Stuart."

Daphne felt her teeth grind. How could he run to Evelyn and Melissa who were strangers, seeking out their protection and love, but couldn't run to the one who loved him with all her heart?

He paused and stared once more at his hands. "Daphne, if I'd told you I was alive, then those people might have come back for both of us. I had no choice but to leave the life I once had with you. I knew also that for me to return to you, a young and beautiful woman, as someone scarred like this — I knew it wouldn't be right."

"What? Do you think I can't take a man who's scarred?"

"Daphne, you wouldn't have been able to take any of my scars. It wasn't just my face. It was my life. And that wasn't a life I wanted you to live."

"So you created another scar instead. Pretending you were dead and allowing me to grieve all these years. Reliving all those memories. Never being able to put away the pictures." She began to heave in distress.

"I'm sorry, Daphne. I wish there were a way I could help you. I only hope you can believe I did it all to protect you. I believe you're alive because of it. We both are alive."

"This is living?" she cried, standing shakily to her feet. The blanket fell on the floor. "You don't know how many times I wanted to die! When I heard what happened, I thought my life was over. And for years, I felt as if I were walking around dead. If only you had told me what happened. We could have gone away together. I would have left everything to be with you, even my father's business."

"Daphne, that nursery was your life. It still is."

"But it wasn't at first. You were." The tears began to roll down her cheeks. "You were everything to me. You were my sun and moon. Maybe I loved you too much. Maybe it was getting in the way of other things. But I know I would have been there for you, if you hadn't kept this from me."

Jack also rose to his feet. "I didn't know that for certain, Daphne. I honestly didn't know if you would be there. I believed after what happened to me, with the burn and everything, it would have been too much of a shock."

"So you're saying that Melissa was better than I was? That she could live with a changed appearance while I couldn't?"

Jack ran a hand through his hair, making it stand on end. "It was different. Melissa cared about someone named Stuart."

"And now you're someone named Jack. Don't you see? No matter what you say, Henry is still dead. As much as you want to, you can't bring him back to life."

Jack stood there quietly, his eyes shifting back and forth as if considering her words. "Then I want to do something new. Even if I'm not the same person, and you aren't either, is there still hope that God might want us together?"

How could he ask her that? She had no idea what God wanted. Right now her life was turned upside down. She didn't even know how to breathe, let alone think and act. Why did life have to be so complicated? Why couldn't there be a manual on what to do when life came crashing down in the most unexpected ways?

"What can we do?" he asked once more. "I love you. Is there any chance we can create something together? Or is it just wishful thinking?"

"There are still wounds to heal," Daphne said, slowly picking up the blanket. "It can't happen overnight. You can't expect to come back and begin where we left off, not after all this time. It's impossible. And I think that's exactly what you hoped to do."

"I had hoped the sparks would be there," he admitted. "That's why I kept myself back for as long as I did after I came here to Virginia. I wanted to see if anything was left. I wanted to see if you remembered Henry, if you were seeing anyone else, or if you had other things in your life. But you and I are so much alike. Trying to get along but seeing the years catch up. Trying to keep going but knowing how fragile life can be. Wondering if love can still happen."

His words shook her to the core. Fresh tears welled up in her eyes. She didn't resist as Jack came and took her in his arms. She knew she was still a fragile plant, unable to thrive where she was. She was as Rodney once described — a plant suffocating in its tiny pot unless she was transplanted soon. And Jack was desperately trying to transplant her.

When she felt his hand gently lift her chin and his eyes stare into hers, a sudden fear swept over her. It had been so long since she had been in another man's arms. He gazed at her with the same intensity she remembered long ago.

Daphne twisted out of his embrace and wiped the tears from her face. "It's getting late."

He nodded, picked up his set of keys from the stand, and said a swift good-bye. Daphne never looked back but kept her head bent, staring at the carpet. *God, please tell me what to do!*

Jack came home that night, torn in his heart and his spirit. *The answer was close, so very close, but I rushed. Look what I've caused all these years, and even now, when she suffered that heart attack. Oh, God, I know I've been selfish. I should have let her go. I should never have returned to Virginia after Melissa died. But it all seemed so perfect, with Evelyn leaving me the vacation home here and so close to where Daphne's nursery was located. And to find out she had never wed, as if she had been waiting all these years for me to return. I thought when she found out who I was she would leap into my arms. But I was shortsighted. She's right. I have been trying to resurrect Henry. Even though I am Henry, I will never be Henry. Henry is gone. He died in the fire. I'm Jack now, Jack McNary, and one whose heart is linked to another. That is the person Daphne must come to love somehow, some way. But I won't push her anymore. I will leave it in Your hands, God.*

CHAPTER 15

Daphne spent the next week searching for answers. She went to church whenever they had services, hoping the pastor would say something that would tell her God's will concerning Jack McNary. She had several of the ladies over for tea one afternoon in the hope of finding answers. Instead, they chatted about their grandchildren and what their families were planning to do for the upcoming summer vacations. All the talk made her feel even more miserable.

On Tuesday, Daphne decided to take a day off from the nursery. She was feeling lonely again and maybe even a bit selfish. One look at the calendar told her the reason why. Today was her birthday. She informed no one about it; she didn't want to make a big deal of it. But to Daphne, it was a big deal. Another year older, and another year of trials and tribulations. She dressed in a comfortable outfit, then paused when she saw the earrings Henry had once given her long ago, the pair she always wore on Tuesdays. She slipped them on, then went to listen to Bible messages on cassette, hoping for words to soothe her soul.

That evening the doorbell rang. Daphne tiptoed to the window and looked down below to see Rodney's car parked out front. What was he doing here? Had he somehow remembered her birthday? She glanced in the mirror, ran a comb through the row of gray bangs on her forehead, and came down the stairs. At least she was grateful for her strength that had returned after the surgery. A visit to the doctor last week confirmed that the pacemaker was doing very well.

Rodney and Melanie stood at the door. "Happy Birthday!" Rodney said with a big grin. He came forward and planted a kiss on her cheek before presenting her with a wrapped gift.

"You didn't need to come here," she said, opening the door wider to allow them in.

"Of course I did. I had to see my mother on her birthday."

Daphne shook her head. "You could use some discipline, too," she said jokingly.

Rodney grinned. "What — are you gonna make me sit on the stairs for coming to see you? That's what my mother used to do to punish me when I was little. These days I guess they call it time-out." He went over and plopped down on the sofa. Melanie headed into the kitchen. She returned a few minutes later, a big grin on her face, singing "Happy Birthday." In her hands, she carried a layer cake decorated with blue roses.

Daphne tried not to cry, but it was difficult, especially when Melanie placed the cake before her on the coffee table. In blue icing were written the words, HAPPY BIRTHDAY, MOM!

"And many more!" Rodney sang, giving her a hug. "Now open your gift."

Daphne took the package from him and sat down. She carefully undid the tape that held the flowered wrapping and opened it. Inside was a digital camera package.

"Time for some new pictures in those albums of yours," Rodney said, folding his arms.

Daphne stared at it. How would she ever operate something like this? She managed a small thank-you before putting the box on the table.

"Don't you like it?"

"I don't know much about cameras."

"This is the same one I have," he said, taking the camera out of the box. "I'll show you how it works. Then you go to the store and use the picture machine to select your prints. Or I can upload them on my laptop and do it from there."

"What? I don't understand a thing you're saying."

"It's simple. We'll go though it step-by-step. I figured you'd need to start filling your albums with new memories."

Daphne shuddered at his words. He must be hinting at her and Jack. Well, there was no future. It was as lifeless as the plants Jack forgot to water.

"In a little under nine months, to be exact," Melanie added.

"Nine months," Daphne repeated. She straightened in her seat as smiles spread across the faces of both Melanie and Rodney.

"That's right — you're gonna be a grandma!" Rodney announced with a laugh.

"Oh, stop it. I'm not your mother."

"Of course you are," Melanie said. "You mean just as much to us as our own mothers did. And we want you to share this special time with us."

"That's wonderful! I'm very happy for you, I must say."

"We just found out the other day," Melanie continued. "I wasn't feeling too good so I took a pregnancy test. I'll tell you, Daphne, there's nothing more exciting than seeing that magic *x* appear in the little window. Rod leaped so high he bumped his head on the doorway. He got a nasty bruise."

"Really now, young man," Daphne said with a chuckle. "You always did do things in excess." Her heart overflowed with joy at the couple's news.

"So it's time for new things," Rodney repeated. "Just like the flowers that are all in bloom, and everything is coming up roses. And, speaking of roses —"

"Rodney found the most gorgeous blue rosebush, Daphne. It came in on one of the shipments while you were in the hospital."

"I'm glad," she told them honestly. "Red and pink are lovely, but there is something about a blue rose that is so unique." She fell silent then. If only she had her own good news to share with the excited couple sitting before her. Instead, she felt like a hollowed-out shell, without hope. Or could it be that God had sent this sweet couple to give her hope? That newness of life is still possible? Just this morning she had read the verse about trusting in the Lord and not leaning on one's understanding. In her own eyes, nothing made sense. Through God's eyes, everything was perfectly planned and would be completed in order, just like a new baby.

After they left, Daphne went over to the drawer of a small table. Inside lay a folded piece of paper with the address and phone number Jack had given her. With shaky fingers, she took it out. In his own hand, he had written where he lived. Spring Mountain Road. She knew where the road was located. She had been in the area a few times over the course of her life. It was a pretty road, too, at the foot of the Blue Ridge Mountains. Maybe a drive would be in order.

After work the next day, Daphne took care of Chubs, then drove off on a special errand, heading straight for the range of mountains looming before her. She rarely went for a drive unless it was to town for groceries or to church, but something stronger was beckoning to her. She decided to obey the feeling that grew inside.

She enjoyed the sight of the Blue Ridge Mountains in all their glory. This area had been her home for as long as she could remember. Even if Henry at one time wanted her to leave Virginia and live in the mountains of Tennessee where he worked, she couldn't bring herself to leave this place. It was part of her. Nothing would take it away. And now God had seen fit to bring Henry back, even if he was a different person. He had returned despite all the obstacles, just to find her. The thought made her smile.

Soon she was winding her way around the curvy road of Route 810. Spring Mountain Road came up on the right. She had no idea what his house looked like but continued on. The road grew steeper, climbing the shoulder of a foothill that guarded the grand Blue Ridge. Suddenly she saw it — the dirt brown truck he always drove, parked before a modest ranch home overlooking the valley. She slammed on the brakes with a terrific shriek, sending the car into a small ditch.

Jack burst out of the house and ran across the lawn. "Are you all right?" came his anxious voice, only to stop short. "Daphne! What are you doing here?"

"I — uh — I was on a drive," she said quickly, too embarrassed to tell him the real reason for the trip. "Now I have to get out of this mess."

"Allow me." He waited for her to exit the driver's seat. She watched as he backed up the vehicle with skill, into his driveway behind his old pickup truck.

For an instant, she wondered what she was

doing here, early in the evening, and at Jack's house, of all places. He looked like an old farmer, dressed in his usual overalls he had worn the first day he came to her nursery. "Actually I came here to find out what you've been doing with all those plants you bought from me," she said.

He cracked a grin and waved his hand. She followed him to the backyard and gasped. The gardens were expertly formed rectangles and looked free of weeds. Tiny plants in picture-perfect rows stood surrounded by mulch. "I don't believe it."

"Did I do something wrong?"

"Of course not. This is simply beautiful." She gazed up into his face to see it shaded by the brim of the straw hat. "I thought you didn't know a thing about plants."

"So they really look all right, then?"

"I should say so. They look extremely healthy."

In the vegetable garden, Jack had already placed cages for the tomatoes. The broccoli heads were full. "I was about ready to cut a head of broccoli. I also cooked up some of my barbecue. Have you eaten dinner?"

Daphne stared at the home behind her, uncertain about what to do.

"There's a small table and chairs on the patio," he added.

She breathed easier and said that, yes, she was hungry. A big smile broke out on Jack's face. He hurried into the house and came out with a knife and, under Daphne's direction, cut off a huge head of broccoli as the vegetable for the meal. While she roamed the property, looking at the thriving apple trees and even the rosebushes that appeared healthier than her own, Jack was in the kitchen finishing dinner. When he called, she returned to find a small table set for two, along with a lit candle. He had also changed clothes.

"I hope you don't mind the candle," he said, "but if it gets dark, we can still see. Unless you don't want to see what you're eating."

"Of course I do." Daphne promptly sat down in the chair he pulled out. She lowered her head while Jack said the blessing, then began eating. Neither of them said anything for a time while they ate, listening to the last call of the birds for the day. The steady hum of insects soon took over as the sun dipped behind the mountains.

"You do have a nice place here," Daphne finally said, wiping her lips on the napkin. "I haven't been back to this area since I was young. Remember Jane Neely? I think she lived down the road not far from here."

"Yes. You said she had a crush on me."

"She did. She never used to say anything to me in high school. For some reason, the word got out that I was seeing some muscular lumberjack from Tennessee. Then she was around the nursery all the time, asking questions." Daphne gazed out over the landscape, watching the daylight melt with the approach of evening. "So this was Evelyn's home?"

"Her vacation home."

"Did you ever come here with Melissa?"

Jack bent over his plate in silence for a moment. When he answered yes, Daphne nodded. "I figured you must have come here for vacations, with this home being in Melissa's family and all."

"It was hard moving here at first after Melissa died," he admitted. "There were many memories. But working in the garden helped. It was good to see life come again after experiencing death — first Melissa's, then Evelyn's. I think I know why you like the nursery so much. Life grows there. And I understand better now why you reacted the way you did when I told you how I killed the first batch of plants."

"I was totally unreasonable that day," she said. "Getting upset over silly little plants." Daphne was thankful the dim light masked her flushed cheeks.

"Daphne, they aren't silly. They are part of God's creation, and His creation is perfect." The look in his eyes softened. "And just the same, you're also part of His creation. As much as I want to be with you, I've decided I'm going to let God determine my future. I know what I would like to have happen. But if it isn't His will, then I'll just be hitting my head against a wall. And I think that's what I've been doing these past few weeks. I've been pretty selfish."

Daphne stared. How could he sit there and say such things when it was she who had thrust up walls and been basking in her own hurt and jealousy?

"I'm glad you came," he added. "I won't deny it. But I won't let it speak for anything either. We can call this a nice visit between friends."

"Is that what you want?" Daphne heard herself say, shocked by her own words. Yet she couldn't help how she felt. If only he would take her in his arms and tell her everything would be fine. If only she would not die alone but leave this world experiencing the love of another.

His head popped up. "What?"

"Do you want to be just friends?"

"Daphne, I want only what's best for us.

And if that means a friendship, that would be fine with me."

"But is that really what you want?" she pressed.

Jack lifted his glass of lemonade and took a long swallow. The glass clinked on the table with resolve. "No. No, it isn't. I don't want to be just friends. I love you. It's a season for new things, just like the gardens I planted. I'm hoping it's also the right time for us, too."

Daphne's heart nearly leaped at these words, the same words she had been sensing in her own heart. Could this be a confirmation from God?

"Look — the moon is beginning to rise." Jack pointed at the faint rays of golden moonlight rising in the east. Daphne turned to look. When she did, she heard a chair scrape. She felt his presence come up behind her and then the feel of his strong hands on her shoulders, gentle, soothing, slowly gliding down her arms. A tingle shot through her like the tingles she had when she was young and in love. She began to shake.

"It's all right," his voice said in a light whisper. "I'm here, and I won't leave you." He came around the chair and knelt before her. He gazed longingly into her eyes.

"Henry —," she said with a sob. She buried her face in his shoulder. The strength of his arms around her was powerful, filling in the empty hole, soothing the ache, healing the wounds. When he kissed her, everything came to life. The planting of long ago had finally sprouted. Peace flowed like the warmth of love in her being. God had answered her prayer.

" 'Love in any language . . . straight from the heart . . . pulls us all together, never apart! And once we learn to speak it, all the world will hear, love in any language, fluently spoken here!' "

Today Daphne felt no animosity toward that beautiful singing voice of her employee. It bounced across the walls of the shop and carried outside to the tables of plants that customers perused on a busy summer day. She even found her foot tapping in time to his song. She knew from the volume of his voice that Rodney was trying his best to irritate her. No more. The rough edges had been made smooth.

Her fingers gently slid the tiny little impatiens into a new pot. When she'd arrived at the nursery that day, she was amazed to find Rodney already there. He had done the morning count and had taken up a broom to sweep out the remnants of dirt and dust from last evening. The sight of it all confirmed her feeling that today was the day. She wasn't exactly sure how to break the news to him. Perhaps if she just came out and said it, the Lord would supply her with the words.

Wiping her hands on a towel, she ventured out of the greenhouse to find Rodney tending to several customers. Everyone turned and smiled in her direction. The warmth of their expressions soothed her heart and soul. When the customers left the store, carrying boxes of plants, Daphne came to the counter. "Everything going all right?"

"Looking good."

"And is Melanie feeling good?"

"I wouldn't exactly call throwing up in the bathroom every morning feeling good. But she knows it's because of the baby, so I guess that's to be expected."

Daphne ran her finger across the smooth counter. How she would miss this place. It had been her home for so long. "I guess it's a good thing then that you will be getting some extra income."

"Babies can be expensive. And Melanie keeps saying we need a bigger place." Rodney let out a sigh. "I'm not sure what to do."

"It's all right." She reached over and patted his hand. He stared back as if surprised by the contact. "Everything is going to be all right. Trust me."

"If you say so."

"I know so." She inhaled a sharp breath before gazing around the store. "I'm going to miss this place so much. But I know it's the best thing to do."

Rodney leaned over the counter, staring in confusion. "Miss Elliot, you're not making any sense."

"Rodney, I'm giving you the business. Today I'm announcing my retirement."

His mouth fell open. "What?"

"I've decided it's time to move on. You were right, you know."

"I was right about what? I can't even begin to imagine."

"That I need a bigger pot in life. This place was causing me to get root-bound. I needed to be transplanted, but I was fighting it tooth and nail. God tried to send people in my path to let me know He wanted to change things. But I didn't want Him to do it. I thought I had it all figured out, but it only made me more miserable. Besides" — she continued to run her finger across the counter — "the doctor thinks it would be good for my heart to leave this place. The stress level hasn't made things better for me."

"But what will you do? I mean, you've been at this place since you were little."

"Ten years old, to be exact. I started as you did, counting seed packets and sweeping out dust with a broom. My, those were the days." She chuckled at the memory of her pigtails flying in the breeze as she helped her father. In the distance, her brother, Charles, would groan about lifting the heavy bags of mulch into their respective stacks. But for Daphne, there was nothing better than working among God's creations of plants and rich earth. It was her calling. Little did she realize, but this place she loved so well kept her until another life called to her.

"How can you just leave? Won't you miss it?"

"I'm sure there will be things I'll miss. That voice of yours, for instance. Meddling in other people's affairs. Trying to run lives." She chuckled, then added with much conviction, "Being a caring young man who loved a mean spinster as he would his mother."

"I hope you aren't doing this out of some need to pay me back. If anything, I should pay you back for all you've done for Melanie and me."

"No, sir, young man. On the contrary, as I said, life has a way of changing. It's time to go work in other gardens."

At that moment, the door to the shop creaked open. The footsteps were solid upon the wooden floor of the shop. Daphne smiled at the vision that walked in, as if the sun had just risen.

"Aha!" Rodney exclaimed in a loud voice. "Now it all makes sense. Have you an announcement to make?"

"Well, not quite," she said, feeling the heat in her cheeks. "Maybe soon."

"Sooner than you think," Jack added, grabbing Rodney's hand and shaking it heartily. "I had to thank you for everything."

"I didn't do anything."

"You did . . . more than you know."

He offered his arm to Daphne who slipped her hand through the crook in his elbow. They moved off toward the door that led to the greenhouse. This had been Daphne's place of joy, the place where she nursed plants until they could find a home with a customer who would care for them with loving hands. Yes, she would miss this place. Maybe she could come back once in a while if Rodney needed a hand, especially when Melanie had the baby. But for now, she was content to walk around, gazing at the workstation still cluttered with potting soil, peat pots, a pair of gardening gloves, and her trowel with the decorative pink handle.

"Are you sorry?" Jack asked.

"I would be sorry if I turned my back on what's ahead of me," she said. "Of course I loved this place very much. My father showed me right here how to transplant seedlings."

"I remember coming here when you had your elbows in dirt, both forty years ago and now." He gently turned her toward him. "And I remember how sad I was when I had to leave and go back to Tennessee to continue on at the lumber mill. But all things work together for good."

Daphne never forgot the day when he took off in his rickety old car, heading back for the woods of Tennessee. When his death was announced, life had taken a turn down some dark alley. Now it had emerged into the light and at the right time. "But you came back."

"When I came back here five years ago to live, there were so many times I wanted to see you and talk to you. I wanted you to know I was alive. I just didn't know how to say it."

"I'll admit I never knew you were Henry,

though there were instances when you reminded me of him. Something in the eyes. During the croquet game. All that dirt on your face. Holding me after the thorns pricked my hands. When you showed me that license, everything made sense. Of course my mind wouldn't accept it at first, but my heart did."

"I almost killed that heart, too," he said mournfully, rubbing her hand.

"No, you gave it new life. If I hadn't fainted that day in the shop, it might have been too late. I could have been here, working with my plants, lonely and miserable, and suffered a heart attack. You never know."

His arms curled around her. "You aren't going to leave me, Daphne. I know one day we'll be called home to be with the Lord, but I want it to happen knowing you were by my side and with a ring on your finger."

"So is this a proposal?" she asked with a laugh.

He reached into his pocket and brought out a box. Daphne gasped. Her heart leaped, not with pain but with joy. She took the box and opened it. The ring was just as she used to dream about, a pretty diamond with her birthstone set on either side. She'd always told Henry she wanted a ring with her birthstone in the setting. *Because if I wasn't born, we wouldn't be engaged!* she used to joke. The sight of the ring brought tears to her eyes. Dear sweet Henry. "Y–you remembered."

He bent over her and kissed her gently. "Yes, I remembered. How could I forget? You were very clear about what you wanted when we talked about it. Could it be forty years ago?"

"Yes, all those years ago. During that time, we both lived different lives."

"We may have grown in different gardens, but we share the same Creator who knew when the time was right to bring us together again." He then became serious. "Daphne, it's forty years later, but will you marry me?"

She glanced at the plants aligned in a row on the workbench, some with flowers that waved from the breeze blowing through the open door. Nodding her head, Daphne took the ring and slipped it onto her left hand. "It's beautiful."

He grinned and offered her his arm. "How about some lunch to celebrate? The Hardware Store Restaurant is running some good specials."

Daphne laughed and hooked her hand through his arm. Like the plants she so lovingly tended, love, too, could bloom at any age.

EPILOGUE

"Under the authority vested in me, I now pronounce you man and wife. What God has joined together, let no man separate. You may now kiss the bride."

The kiss was marvelous, the lips tender as they found hers, just as she envisioned it would be. Then suddenly he kissed her again, prompting a round of laughter from the congregation that rose to the very rafters of the church. Daphne couldn't help but laugh herself. What a strange sound to hear — laughter from her lips that so often criticized or spoke words of sadness and depression. Today she felt sprightly, ready to face the world for another forty years, even as they turned to greet the enthusiastic congregation, ready to present themselves as Mr. and Mrs. Jack McNary. They stepped off the platform, arm in arm, to the cheers and smiles from those Daphne had come to know. Loyal customers of the nursery.

Friends. Her doctor. And to her surprise, an older man with a craggy face and graying hair but familiar nonetheless. Her older brother, Charles.

Daphne inhaled a swift breath and went at once to embrace him. He seemed startled by the greeting. Despite their estranged past, Daphne felt nothing but happiness that he had come all this way from California to be here.

Suddenly she saw the tears in his tired eyes. "I'm sorry for everything, Daphne," he mumbled.

"You're sorry . . . ?" she began. "You don't have anything to be sorry for."

"Yes, I have. For many things. Most of all, for not being there when you needed me. I hold nothing but admiration for you. And I'm happy that everything turned out for you in the end." He reached over to shake Jack's hand. "I have to admit, your story has been a shock to me. Maybe I can talk with you more about it sometime."

"Please do," Daphne said, gripping his arm. "It really is a miracle of God. It taught me so much about how He cares for us, in the small and the large things. But I'm so glad you're here, Charles. You can't know."

His smile warmed Daphne's heart, even as she and Jack walked the remainder of the way down the aisle. When they reached the rear of the sanctuary, a high-pitched wail greeted them. Melanie was there, trying desperately to calm her two-month-old baby girl, Rose. Daphne couldn't help the tears that sprang to her eyes. "And how is my dear grandbaby?" she said, reaching over to give the infant a kiss.

Melanie smiled. "You may regret having invited her to your wedding, Daphne."

"Nonsense. Even if she isn't my blood relation, I still consider her mine." She handed Jack her bouquet of blue-tinted roses and took the little baby in her arms. All at once, the crying stopped and the tiny crook of a smile formed on her wee face.

"Daphne, you have a way about you that makes everyone smile," Jack said with a chuckle. "Even the littlest ones."

"It wasn't always that way, you know. I'm happy God doesn't give up on us. And He didn't give up, did He?"

Jack kissed her on the ear. "No, He didn't. And I am so glad you didn't give up on me either."

"I thought you might get a few comments on the dress you're wearing," Melanie said, taking little Rose back in her arms. "Most brides wear white. But you always had your own ideas, Daphne."

Daphne looked down at her midnight blue dress that once hung in the back closet for years upon years, only to be resurrected for this special occasion. "My dear girl, how could I not wear this dress? You remember it, Jack."

"Of course I remember it. You wore it to our first ball forty years ago. And the pearls to match."

"It needed fixing up, but with my sickness and all last year, I had no trouble fitting into it. I guess there is some good that can come out of being sick and getting a pacemaker. I never would have thought I could wear the dress again."

Melanie laughed, linking her arm through Daphne's as they proceeded toward the church hall and the reception. All at once, Rodney came out from behind the door and presented them with a huge Mylar balloon. "Happy Wedding Day to you!" he sang.

"What mischief are you up to now, young man?" On the balloon was the head of a smiling Bambi along with the word CONGRATULATIONS.

"Don't you remember? You were quoting Bambi to me one day in the nursery, calling love a pain in the pinfeathers. I just had to get it."

"You do beat all," Daphne said. "What

would I do without you?"

"Admit it. Life would get boring. But you must be a little happy how the nursery business is going."

"You mean getting a front-page news story about it in the lifestyle section of the *Progress* this past Sunday? Yes, I am very happy. Everything has worked out, beyond my dreams." *Everything,* she thought, watching Jack as he went over to speak to the minister of his church and some church friends. At that moment, he looked over at her. She threw him a kiss. He smiled, raised his hand and caught it, just like those times long ago. The scar on his face disappeared. He was Henry again, with his twinkling eyes and youthful appearance. He was all hers, to have and to hold, from this day forward.

When Rodney turned on the music and a waltz from long ago filled the room, Jack came forward and swept her up in his arms. "You still remember how to dance, don't you?" he asked.

"Oh, dear. I'm not so sure. That was a very long time ago."

It came to her easily, as if she had been doing this all her life rather than forty years ago. Maybe the dress sparked the memory. Or the excitement of the wedding. Or simply the man whose arm cradled her while his free hand led her across the linoleum flooring of the reception room. Rodney saluted them with a glass of bubbly apple-flavored beverage.

"You're having no trouble remembering," Jack noted with appreciation. "It looks like you have been doing this for years."

"I have," she confessed, "in my memories. But now I can live it. We can have new memories with a love that never really went away."

"Ageless, just like you."

Daphne had to laugh. "No, I am older. But not too old at least to dance."

"Or for love."

Resting her head against his firm shoulder as the music enveloped them, Daphne couldn't help but agree.

The employees of Thorndike Press hope you have enjoyed this Large Print book. All our Thorndike and Wheeler Large Print titles are designed for easy reading, and all our books are made to last. Other Thorndike Press Large Print books are available at your library, through selected bookstores, or directly from us.

For information about titles, please call:
    (800) 223-1244

or visit our Web site at:
    www.gale.com/thorndike
    www.gale.com/wheeler

To share your comments, please write:
    Publisher
    Thorndike Press
    295 Kennedy Memorial Drive
    Waterville, ME 04901